Canceled Memories

Middle East Literature in Translation
Michael Beard *and* Adnan Haydar, *Series Editors*

Selected Titles from Middle East Literature in Translation

A Brave New Quest: One Hundred Modern Turkish Poems
    Talat S. Halman, trans. and ed., Jayne L. Warner, assoc. ed.

A Child from the Village
    Sayyid Qutb; John Calvert and William Shepard, eds. and trans.

Contemporary Iraqi Fiction: An Anthology
    Shakir Mustafa, ed. and trans.

Distant Train: A Novel
    Ibrahim Abdel Megid; Hosam Aboul-Ela, trans.

I, Anatolia and Other Plays: An Anthology of Modern Turkish Drama, Volume Two
    Talat S. Halman and Jayne L. Warner, eds.

İbrahim the Mad and Other Plays: An Anthology of Modern Turkish Drama, Volume One
    Talat S. Halman and Jayne L. Warner, eds.

The Journals of Sarab Affan: A Novel
    Jabra Ibrahim Jabra; Ghassan Nasr, trans.

My Thousand and One Nights: A Novel of Mecca
    Raja Alem and Tom McDonough

Sleeping in the Forest: Stories and Poems
    Sait Faik; Talat S. Halman, ed., and Jayne L. Warner, assoc. ed.

Thieves in Retirement: A Novel
    Hamdi Abu Golayyel; Marilyn Booth, trans.

Canceled Memories

a novel

Nazik Saba Yared

Translated from the Arabic by Nadine Sinno

Syracuse University Press

English translation copyright © 2009 by Syracuse University Press
Syracuse, New York 13244-5160

All Rights Reserved

First Edition 2009

09 10 11 12 13 14   6 5 4 3 2 1

Originally published in Arabic as *Al-Dhikrayat al-mulghat* (Beirut: Nawfal, 1998).

The paper used in this publication meets the minimum requirements of American National Standard for Information Sciences—Permanence of Paper for Printed Library Materials, ANSI Z39.48–1984.∞™

For a listing of books published and distributed by Syracuse University Press, visit our Web site at SyracuseUniversityPress.syr.edu.

ISBN-13: 978-0-8156-0937-7   ISBN-10: 0-8156-0937-X

Library of Congress Cataloging-in-Publication Data

Yarid, Nazik Saba.

[Dhikrayat al-mulghah. English]

Canceled memories : a novel / Nazik Saba Yared ; translated from the Arabic by Nadine Sinno.

p. cm. — (Middle East literature in translation)

ISBN 978-0-8156-0937-7 (hardcover : alk. paper)

I. Sinno, Nadine. II. Title.

PJ7874.A77D4513 2009

892.7'36—dc22

200804873

Manufactured in the United States of America

Contents

Translator's Acknowledgments

vii

Canceled Memories

1

NAZIK SABA YARED is an acclaimed Lebanese writer and critic. Her critical publications include studies on the poetry of classical and modern poets, such as Abu Nawas, Ibn al-Rumi, Ahmad Shawqi, Elias Abu Shabaka, Hammad Ajrad, and Gibran Kahlil Gibran. Her book *Al-Rahhâlûn al-Arab wa-hadârat al-gharb fi al-nahda al-'Arabîyah al-Haditha* (1992) was translated into English as *Arab Travelers and Western Civilization* in 1996. Her book *Secularism and the Arab World*, written in English, was published in 2002. Her fiction includes *Nuqtat al-dâ'ira* (Center of the Circle, 1983); *Al-Sadâ al-makhnûq* (The Stifled Echo, 1986); *Kana al-ams ghadan* (Yesterday Was Tomorrow, 1988); *Taqasim 'ala watar dâd'i'* (1992), which was translated into English as *Improvisations on a Missing String* by Stuart A. Hancox in 1997; *Fi dhill al-qal'ah* (In the Shadow of the Citadel, 1996); *Al-Dhikrayat al-mulghat* (Canceled Memories, 1998); and *Al-Aqni'a* (The Masks, 2004). Her autobiography, *Dhikrayat lam taktamil* (Incomplete Memoirs), was published in 2008.

NADINE SINNO is a Ph.D. candidate in comparative literature and an instructor of world literature and English as a second language at the University of Arkansas, Fayetteville. She received an MA in English literature from the American University of Beirut and an MFA in literary translation from the University of Arkansas. She is currently working on her dissertation, tentatively titled "Disrupted Places, Creative Spaces: The Politics of Transformation in Contemporary Arab Women's Fiction." Her work has been published in *Representing Minorities: Studies in Literature and Criticism,* edited by Larbi Touaf and Soumia Boutkhil (2006), and in *Feminism and War: Confronting U.S. Imperialism,* edited by Robin L. Riley, Chandra Talpade Mohanty, and Minnie Bruce Pratt (2008).

Translator's Acknowledgments

THIS TRANSLATION would not have been possible if it were not for the support offered by so many people. I thank Dr. Nazik Saba Yared for trusting me with her novel and for making herself available for any questions throughout this project. Many thanks to Dr. John DuVal, my MFA director, for his encouragement, tireless commitment, and excellent feedback on the entire manuscript. I am deeply indebted to Dr. Adnan Haydar for introducing me to Dr. Yared and for being on my MFA thesis committee as well. I also thank Dr. Miller Williams for teaching me how to be faithful to the spirit of the original text and for encouraging me to read my translation out loud. Josh Capps read many drafts of the manuscript and provided valuable contributions.

I extend my deep gratitude to my fellow translators at the University of Arkansas, especially Annaliese Hoehling, Starla Ling, and Ghadir Zannoun for their insightful comments in our translation workshops and beyond. I am also thankful to my dear friend Michele McKee for her support and meticulous assistance with formatting the manuscript. I am very grateful to the King Fahd Center for Middle East Studies and the Department of English at the University of Arkansas for their continued support of my academic endeavors. Many thanks to Mary Selden Evans and Marcia Hough of Syracuse University Press for their professionalism, efficiency, and kindness.

Finally, I thank Susan Brown, Patty Hays, Lucia Volk, Suze Dambreville, Jason Miller, Bwalya Lungu, and Sarah Gibson for believing in me and cheering me on from beginning to end. A special thanks go to my family, especially my mother, May, for her unconditional love and support over the years.

Her experiences and triumphs during the Lebanese Civil War continue to inform my personal and professional life. Dr. Yared's novel is a testament to the admirable resilience that she and many other Lebanese women displayed in those years.

Canceled Memories

— 1 —

HUDA SET UP HER CAMERA, steadying it on the tripod. She estimated the distance to the church, adjusted the lens, and put on a filter just right for the sunny April day. Then she pressed the button, turned her camera a little bit, and pressed again. Pointing the lens upward, she pressed a third time. She turned her camera right and left and kept pressing, taking pictures of the present. *Lebanon: The Land of Hospitality*—in the past. She remembered the title of the book as she took pictures, fixing her eyes first on the church and then on the camera. She wanted her pictures to be clear, accurate, funny, artistic. Maybe she too could compile these pictures in a book that would include some historical information. Her book, however, wouldn't be about the land of hospitality, she thought bitterly as she picked up her camera and walked toward the church.

She recalled the pictures from that tourist book: the 'Ayn Mrayseh houses with their red roof tiles; the Hôtel Saint Georges with the sea waves rocking against its walls, spraying the white sailboats on the docks, the steam-driven boats awaiting the water skiers, and the white chaises longues lined up, ready to receive the tanned bodies. Overlooking all of this was the Terrace Saint Georges, the gathering place for elegant ladies, businessmen, politicians, journalists, tourists, and spies. Across from the picture of the Hôtel Saint Georges was that of the Phoenicia Hotel, whose top floors housed the city's most popular restaurants and whose bottom floors were home to al-Tawoos al-Ahmar, Le Bain Rouge, its dance floor crowded with dancers. Pictures. More pictures. A past of which only pictures remained and a present of which only pictures—like hers, for example— and the memory will remain.

Standing at the threshold of the church, she remembered *The Land of Hospitality* again. It used to bother her that the church doors were closed except for the scheduled hours of prayer. Now there was no door to keep the people out. "The house of God welcomes everybody," the church's pockmarked walls and empty doorway seemed to be saying. Huda responded to the invitation, crossed the threshold, and stepped inside. A dreadful emptiness dazed her. The benches and chairs were gone. A roof tile and broken pieces of wood lay in place of the altar. Her eyes roamed over the punctured walls and pillars. Even the bombs and missiles could not shake those pillars, only crack them here and there. Her gaze was met with rooflessness—the blue sky. The sons of the land of hospitality wouldn't allow a barrier between man and God, so they blew off the ceiling.

⸻ ⸻ The church was full of people. Faces faded, swam, disappeared in the fog of my anxiety. My arm trembled as I clutched Dad's. It fell. Another arm locked elbows with mine, pressing. I felt a tender power moving it. As we crossed the threshold of the church, I felt people staring at me, scrutinizing my dress, my face, my jewelry. Although my eyes were fixed on the floor, I could feel those eyes. We were met by the white ribbon, which stood as a barrier, forbidding people from walking up the aisles before the bride arrived. His hands stretched out to hold mine. Together we untied the ribbon blocking the way. Together we continued walking, slowly, toward the altar and the waiting bishop. I couldn't make out what the bishop—or priest?—was saying. Figures disappeared behind the incense; words disappeared behind the thoughts, the dreams of the future.

⸻ ⸻ Huda went back to her camera. She readjusted for the distance, the frames, the light, and the shade and took more pictures. She looked at her watch, then packed the camera in her big black bag, folded the tripod, and left the church.

Two burned-out stores stood across the street. Although the first store's sign was riddled with holes, the bullets had failed to erase the name. The sign, in Western characters, read "Bouquet." The other store's rusty, worn-out sign was also in Western characters; it read "Mode Bébé." A florist and a babies' fashionable clothing shop, spelled out all in French. Foreign products are of course the best, Huda thought as she smiled cynically and looked back at the road.

Where did that young woman come from? Young woman? A child stood in front of her, extending a bouquet of flowers for her to buy: daisies, red anemones, and mountain flowers. A basket of flowers lay before the child's bare feet. Huda stared at the little feet. Layers of dirt didn't conceal the bruises.

"It's just a thousand liras, ma'am," the child said. "Take one for your sweetheart." Huda smiled. If only the child knew who her sweetheart was and what had become of him. Noticing the smile on Huda's face, the child felt more confident in selling her flowers.

"How about three for two thousand?" she said, extending three bouquets. Huda laughed. In this country, even children knew the art of business! She studied the child's bright, imploring eyes, the dimple on her right cheek, the thick black hair, half-covered with a scarf that had been white in the remote past.

"So, what do you think, ma'am?"

A businessperson's time is precious! Huda opened her bag slowly without taking her eyes off the tiny body with its faded floral dress and bare feet. She put her hand inside her bag and asked the child, "What's your name?"

"Sana."

"That's a beautiful name," she said. "Do you have any brothers or sisters? A father? A mother?"

The hand had been extended with flowers suddenly withdrew. The child's eyes were now filled with fear and anger instead of helplessness.

"Bitch!" the girl yelled at Huda. "You making fun of me?"

She picked up her basket, turned her back on Huda, and walked away with her head held high. Huda stood in her place, contemplating the tiny body scurrying away in spite of its burden. She recalled the news she had been reading in the morning papers: $500 million for a road from Hadath to al-Masnaa'; $191 million for the streets of Beirut; and $650 million for the reconstruction of Beirut. The same newspapers had been reporting the news of those who were going to enjoy the bright future in "the land of compassion":

> Fadia—eleven years old. After her father died, her mother married a man who asked her to contribute to the family income. She met some kids who

worked for a man who provided young men with girls, by making the girls sell gum or bread, or just by hanging around on the streets. Fadia had approached a car, offered her bread for sale, and asked the guy drinking beer if he'd like a young woman to keep him company.

Samar—twelve-years old. Her neighbor once saw her leaving a young man's house and counting her money. Then she went into a grocery store and bought some chocolate and fruit. The investigation revealed that her neighbors had a lot of negative things to say about her. Samar's father constantly beat her, and her mother insisted that the little girl bring in money in any possible way. Samar said, "When I was a child, a stranger came to our house. I saw him with my mother in a weird position. After that, my mother hated me and started being cruel to me. My father and mother team up against me. She's always telling him that I disobey her, so he hates me too and treats me cruelly."

The security men marched into a house where prostitution and homosexual activities were going on.... The police investigation revealed that the people operating the network employed minor girls as prostitutes and offered other services such as providing men with little boys for a fee from a hundred to two hundred dollars.

The newspapers had nothing to say about the future of Fadia, Samar, and the other minors. Did Sana belong to that category of minors? Was that why she got upset at my innocent question and ran away angry and frightened? Then Huda remembered something. She looked at her watch and hurried to Riyad al-Sulh Square, where she had parked her car.

"Dina must think I've forgotten about her," she thought as she got into the car and started the engine. The image of Dina replaced that of Sana. Then Sana came back, and the two images blended. Huda could see her daughter's scared, angry eyes. She could see Dina, crouched quietly in the corner, looking and listening for a few minutes before closing her eyes and covering her ears with her hands. Huda would catch a glimpse of her daughter and lower her voice. She'd look at Sharif and shake her head slightly, pointing at Dina. In turn, he'd lower his voice, and the storm would subside.

➤ ➤ Dina was waiting for Huda in front of her school.

"What took you so long?" Dina asked before Huda had even opened the door for her.

"What are your plans for tomorrow?" Huda asked, replying with another question. "I was thinking maybe we could go see a movie today."

"What movie?"

"You choose."

Huda kept her eyes on the road as she listened to Dina listing movies and her friends' opinions on them—their strengths and weaknesses. *Lorenzo's Oil* is beautiful and touching, considering that the movie's based on a true story, but it's sad. Jodi Foster's performance in *Silence of the Lambs* is outstanding, but the movie is scary.

"How about a piano concert instead? It—"

"No way."

Huda knew what her daughter was about to say: classical music is for old people, not teenagers. None of her friends like classical music. It's so outdated. Huda had tried convincing her many times that art—real art—is timeless and that the best musicians had become stars when they were still teenagers or even children. She had tried telling Dina that she should be more independent and have her own taste, instead of being constantly influenced by her friends. Dina would listen to her go on and on and finally say, "That's my business." Had she raised Dina herself, would Dina still have had that attitude? That response?

When they arrived home, Huda parked the car in the garage and took the bag with the camera out of the trunk.

"The power's out, as usual," Dina said. "Why do you live on the sixth floor?"

Huda didn't answer as she slowly climbed the stairs.

"Thank God Grandma's on the first floor of her building."

When they got to the sixth floor, Huda opened the door, put her things in her room, and went into the kitchen to make dinner.

"Dina, we'll have dinner before the movies. You go ahead with your homework while I make it."

"Tomorrow's Saturday. I can do my homework tomorrow." The answer came from the living room, and Huda heard the sound of the TV. How could her daughter make studying plans for Saturday—the only day Huda could get to spend with her? And only twice a month? Could she blame her daughter's attitude on the fact that she was a typical teenager? Or was it, as they said, a case of "out of sight, out of mind"?

"We're not staying home tomorrow," she said. "I have cool plans."

"What plans?"

Huda was pleased that her daughter was interested. "It's a surprise. I'm not telling."

When Dina didn't say anything else, Huda assumed her daughter had started studying—reluctantly. Am I right? Wrong? What has become of us in "the land of enlightenment and civilization," not just "the land of compassion"? she wondered as she chopped the onions.

⸺ ⸺ "Hi, Jawad," I said leading him into the living room. "Long time no see. We missed you." Then I called Sharif. "Guess who's here?" I looked at Jawad out of the corner of my eyes. A fashionable gray suit and an expensive tie. I didn't dare think about how much it must have cost, just as I didn't dare ask about the reasons for his long absence. Why scratch the wound? When Sharif came in, I couldn't help but notice his shirt's worn collar, the style of his jacket showing its age. The two friends hugged, and I went into the kitchen to make coffee. The phone rang, and I heard Sharif's voice.

"I can't," he said. "What's the point?" A few minutes later he said, "Okay," in exasperation.

When I came back with the coffee, Sharif was standing, apologizing to Jawad. "I'm sorry. It's an urgent meeting. I have to be there." Then he left.

"You may as well drink your coffee before you leave," I called after him. He didn't answer, and I heard the door shut behind him. I handed Jawad his cup and sat across from him, silently sipping my coffee. He passed me a magazine with a bright cover: it was a picture of him standing in front of some bookshelves. I studied the picture for a second, and before I could say anything, he said, "They interviewed me. My childhood, my family, my studies, my work."

So that's the purpose of your visit after the long absence, to flaunt your fame and power, I said to myself. I remained silent, studying the picture. I opened the magazine. Was my silence bothering him?

"Naturally, I mentioned my friends, especially you and Sharif. You know how much I used to admire him . . . and you."

I didn't miss the fact that he had used the past tense. My anger rose.

"Who didn't admire Sharif?" I said, ignoring the last part of his sentence. I asked myself for the thousandth time if Jawad had ever truly admired Sharif or had simply feigned admiration in order to conceal his envy—his feelings of insecurity for needing his distinguished friend's help. I remembered the long hours Sharif used to spend with him, explaining a complicated law, pointing out the verdicts that applied or didn't apply, and the reasons for their consistency or inconsistency with that law. We used to study at my house because, as Sharif used to say, it was the quietest place. Me with my history books, my fiancé and his friend with their law books. His friend became my friend too. Together we were like a trinity—far from being holy of course. You couldn't spot one of us without the others . . . until life toppled the standards of excellence or rather what people consider "excellent."

"You must have benefited a lot from his friendship, from his explanations when you couldn't figure things out on your own," I said, unable to control myself. Did he sense the resentment in my comment?

He said nonchalantly, "I've never denied the good things he did for me. On the contrary, it hurts me that he didn't get what he really deserved out of life."

I went to the kitchen to get the box of cookies—or rather to keep my tongue from lashing out at him. I had wanted to reply, "Because Sharif is honest with himself, he never settled for being a hypocrite like you. Unlike you, he didn't leach onto his sect in order to be appointed its spokesperson so he could pursue his self-interests in its name. Unlike you, he refused to suck up to influential people, to never miss a party in honor of some hotshot so that the newspapers would get a snap of him pausing next to that hotshot. He didn't show up at every conference and seminar and take part in every debate." Despite my contempt for Jawad's opportunism, I was impressed by his ability to grab every chance to get interviewed, to be on a radio show, to appear on TV so people would know him and his reputation would spread. He was always the one sent as a representative to the Conference of Arab Lawyers in Cairo. He got invited to the Francophone Conference in Paris, to meetings in London, the United States, Stockholm.

I extended to him the box of cookies.

"Actually, I should be watching my weight," he said, but he stretched out his hand and grabbed two.

"It must be the numerous feasts you get invited to." Neither my tone of voice nor my smile could conceal my sarcasm.

"I wish I could get away from all that, Huda," he explained. "I wish I could live like you and Sharif, in peace and—"

I laughed. He was actually trying to hide his contempt for us, his pity, behind a facade of admiration.

"Jawad, you can never be like us . . . like Sharif."

Did Sharif's father choose that name as a good omen, or did Sharif get so affected by his name that he turned out to be an honest person? And Jawad? He was indeed generous. He never came back from any of his trips without a present for Dina, a toy or a dress. He always had a present for me too: French perfume, a silk scarf, expensive accessories we couldn't afford. I'd blush, wondering if I should say no to his gifts. Jawad would look at Sharif, insisting that I accept them. I'd look at Sharif helplessly.

"Come on, Huda," Sharif used to say. "Jawad is like a brother to me." Did his dignity prevent him from saying anything else? Did his disinterest in money make him indifferent to the value of those gifts? Did he forget what Jawad had tried to do? Or did he really feel that there was no difference between him and Jawad? With a lump in my throat, I finally would accept the gifs, for Sharif's sake . . . and mine.

Jawad reached for the box of cookies and grabbed two more. I started talking again, hoping he wouldn't understand what I really meant.

"We're not rich like you, or famous," I said, "but Sharif is content. He believes in the value of his work, its spiritual value."

"I can't see how an administrative job in the government can satisfy someone like Sharif."

The sound of his teeth crushing the cookie crushed me too. "He got a job with the government because of the guaranteed pay. After all, he's got a family to take care of, not to mention his mother," I said indignantly. "Besides, who told you he's dissatisfied with his job? He used to always win the government's cases against corrupt contractors. He's saved the government hundreds of thousands of liras."

"What about himself? What did he save for himself? A good reputation? Does his good reputation pay your bills?" he asked, his eyes roaming around the room. His condescension was apparent in the tone of voice and in the smile that made his lips arch. Was he actually comparing our worn, simple furniture to the fancy furniture of his house? His sarcasm, his silent contempt, infuriated me.

"We're content," I said. "Money isn't everything."

He brushed the cookie crumbs off his jacket and pants and got up from his seat. Was he trying to control his anger? He stood before me and put his heavy arm on my shoulders.

"Huda, don't get upset," Jawad said. "I appreciate Sharif. I admire his integrity, his honesty with himself. What matters is that he's content." His tone of voice—although still condescending—pleaded for reconciliation. He remained silent for a moment and then said, "If you ever need anything, you know I'm here."

His arm on my shoulders prevented me from moving, from getting up. I wanted to end that unpleasant confrontation, to shake off my feelings of hurt and humiliation. Need him? For what? I didn't say anything. At the time, it didn't occur to me that our need for him would be the cause of my downfall. My gaze fell on his fancy magazine. I picked it up and leafed through its pages until I got to the interview of him. He took his arm off my shoulder, and I skimmed over the questions and answers.

"Congratulations, Jawad," I said. "Although we know everything you've said here"—and haven't said, I thought—"we'll read it with pleasure because we're proud of you and of our friendship." I stood up and said good-bye. Was I less of a hypocrite than he was? I didn't want him to leave with the memory of my anger, giving him the pleasure of knowing that I was envious, heartbroken, and regretful.

Regretful? No. But wasn't I heartbroken? When we were students, we used to dream about defending justice, about making justice win the way it did in movies when a bright lawyer would defend a cause. We participated in many demonstrations in defense of the truth. We went on strikes demanding justice. Jawad was at the head of all those demonstrations. He was one of the most enthusiastic activists. Then we left the university world, the world of hopes, dreams, and movies, and Sharif got a job.

When did my enthusiasm for listening to him disappear—for listening to him discuss his findings after doing his legal research, the violations he discovered after reviewing new regulations published in the official paper and the legal opinions of the most competent lawyers in cases similar to his? It mattered to me that he discovered fraud, that he brought forth compelling evidence and cogent arguments to prove his case. Together we rejoiced every time he succeeded at uncovering any violation on the part of some contractor. Together we were under the illusion that he was contributing to the government's progress by making it capable of discovering fraud and putting an end to it, that he was helping develop the country so that only the good projects would be carried out.

When did I become disillusioned? When did my interest, my enthusiasm, wane? Suddenly? Gradually? I don't know. All I know is that I started just to half-listen to him. After a while, I turned a completely deaf ear to him. Was it because I became preoccupied with other things: Dina's birth, her vaccination appointments, the rising prices, and of course the war? Or was it because Sharif, too, was getting disgusted? Without hiding his disgust, he'd say sadly at first, "The important cases don't get sent to me. They get transferred to employees who I know are less accurate and careful." Later, he'd bitterly explain, "They transfer them to someone willing to bend the rules according to how much the defendant offers." His bitterness turned into despair when his job became limited to writing routine reports or dealing with cases that didn't involve gaining, losing, or squandering large sums of money. With time, his despair developed into apathy.

His attitude infuriated and repulsed me. It didn't matter to him anymore that his boss would bypass him and transfer a transaction to someone willing to overlook any violations. It didn't matter to him that his friends became rich while we kept running after the dime. It didn't matter to him that paying the doctor's fees or buying clothes for our growing child became a concern and that having another baby would be a catastrophe.

I decided to get a job.

"Get a job?" he asked. "What can you do with a history degree?" The tone of his question showed his contempt.

I thought for a second, then said, "I can teach. Schools are always looking for teachers."

"I suppose your huge teacher's salary would cover the expenses of a maid for the housework, the cost of the presentable wardrobe you're going to need, and the salary of whoever will take care of Dina. And the rest of your salary would probably allow us to lead a fancy lifestyle."

His sarcasm got to me. "Dina will be in kindergarten. I'll arrange my schedule around hers. I'll do the housework. I won't hire a maid."

"And then you'll be too exhausted to put up with Dina or me."

"If you're too worried about my getting exhausted, why don't you help me with the housework?"

His sarcastic laugh grew louder. "Imagine me in the kitchen apron, trying to scoop out the inside of a squash and breaking it in two, or trying to make rice and ending up with a salty mess."

"You don't have to cook. You can help me with the dishes or with cleaning the house."

"So I can become the laughingstock of the neighborhood? So they can call me 'Sharifa, the lady of the house'? No, dear. I didn't get married just to end up doing the housework. These are your duties. You may not be satisfied with the money I make, but I am."

I knew perfectly well that he wasn't satisfied and that his loss of interest in his work—his apathy—proved that. But I wasn't satisfied either, so I started looking for a teaching job.

In October, I was hired as a history teacher for the intermediate classes. It was my first step. The salary was small, but it paid for Dina's kindergarten tuition fees and the costs of the additional outfits I needed.

A colleague of mine was pursuing a graduate degree. "If I get a Ph.D., I can teach at the university and make more money," she told me once.

"Is the purpose of education making more money, or is it learning?" I asked without thinking.

"Why can't it be both?"

Her answer made sense to me, so I took the next step and enrolled at the university. I'd wake up at five in the morning and not go to bed before midnight so Sharif wouldn't accuse me of neglecting Dina or my housework. I hid exhaustion behind a silence that was met with Sharif's own silence and sullenness.

One time I was sitting down to my books when he came back from visiting his mother. He slid his index finger on the dining-room table and grumbled. "Haven't you noticed all this dust?"

"Go ahead and sweep it yourself if it bothers you," I replied in the same tone. "I clean only on Saturdays." I wondered if his mother's remarks had something to do with his sudden interest in the dusty furniture.

Another time he came back from visiting a friend. "Khalil invited us over for dinner," he said. "Of course I said no. How can we return their invitation when your majesty is busy teaching and studying?"

I controlled myself and said, "We can invite them over during the holidays or in the summer." He didn't reply, but he neither accepted anybody's invitation nor invited anyone over.

One day Dina was sick. I took her temperature—101 degrees. Her ear was hurting too, so I called the doctor and set up an appointment for the next afternoon.

"Can you stay with her until noon?" I asked Sharif.

"Why should I?" he said. "Because your teaching is more important than my sterile job at the ministry?" His sarcasm was a cover for his feelings of depression. Without saying anything, I called my mother to come and stay with Dina.

Sometimes I tried to break the ice with news from school. "Can you imagine, Sharif? A fifteen-year-old girl was taken out of school by her parents, who wanted to marry her off. They said her time had come. Poor girl," I said, "how can she take up the responsibility of raising children when she's still a child herself? She's going to regret it. Her parents will regret it, too, after it's too late."

Emerging out of his silence, he said, "Who says she's going to regret it? She might be very happy with a husband who'll make a nice life for her."

I understood what he meant, and I shut up.

I told him about the student I punished because he was always cheating. I had sent for his mother and asked her if her son might be cheating because of his fear of his parents' threats and punishments.

"Can you imagine what the respectable lady told me?" I asked. "She said, 'My son is as dumb as a bag of hammers. I told him a thousand times to watch out so the teacher doesn't catch him.'" Sharif didn't comment. He picked up his newspaper, so I understood. Where had *his* honesty gotten him? Perhaps the woman was right.

I'd finish my housework and work on my students' notebooks or my readings and research. The battles that broke out from time to time forced us to stay in our apartment or in our building's bomb shelter, so I used those opportunities to catch up on my reading or writing.

One time I came home angry and bewildered. I waited until Dina was in her room to tell him my story.

"Look what the war has done to us," I said. "A mother came today and asked to see me. When I came into the conference room, she stood up but kept her head down and remained silent. She didn't say anything even when I asked her what the problem was. Tears were running down her cheeks—"

"Someone from her family must've been kidnapped or killed," Sharif interrupted.

"Not at all," I said. "After a long hesitation, she made me swear not to tell anyone—"

"And you're telling me after she made you swear not to?" he interrupted me again.

"I can tell you," I said, ignoring his sarcasm. "You don't know her. Her daughter Rania is my student. She's fifteen. She got pregnant, and she won't say who the guy was. The mother is on the verge of losing her mind, and she doesn't know what to do."

"What can she do?" His tone of irritation surprised me since he didn't know either the girl or her daughter. "What can she do?" he repeated. "She should have taken better care of her daughter earlier. It's the parents, the mothers, who neglect their children because they're outside the house, at—"

"School? University?" I yelled in his face, completing his sentence for him. "I know what you're implying. Dina is a child, but when have I ever neglected her? When have I ever left her alone for a moment?"

"But you can neglect me, leave me alone for hours, days, months," he said. "I want to talk to you, but you're busy correcting homework. I want to invite the neighbors over, but you're getting ready for a test. I want to rest after lunch, but the chairs are lifted onto the bed because your royal highness has no other time to clean the room." The anger and bitterness in his voice stunned me. He stomped away, and I heard the apartment door slam violently. Then I saw Dina coiled up, silent. She had followed the scenario with her eyes and ears, then closed her eyes and covered her ears.

— 2 —

"ARE YOU DONE WITH YOUR BREAKFAST?" Huda asked when Dina pushed her plate away. "Are you full?"

"Yes . . . so what's this nice surprise you've arranged for today?" Dina asked.

"Did you finish your homework? Until you do, I'm not going to tell you anything."

Dina looked at her, puzzled. "I told you yesterday I finished everything before we went to the movies. You don't believe me?" Huda felt ashamed. Was the separation between her and Dina the reason she was misjudging her daughter? Was it Dina's fault? Hers? Sharif's? Jawad's? Whose fault was it?

She shook off these questions and said, "Of course, I believe you. I just forgot I had asked you already. I'm sorry, Dina. Come on, let's go." She started clearing away the dishes and carrying them to the kitchen.

"You still haven't told me your surprise," Dina said. She started washing the dishes while Huda put the leftovers in the fridge.

"We're going downtown," Huda said. "To the Burj Square. Yesterday I was there taking pictures—"

Her daughter's bewildered look stopped her.

Dina quit washing the dishes. "What kind of surprise is that?" she asked. "Looking at damaged buildings and burned-out stores!"

Her daughter's sarcasm angered her.

"Don't you want to see them before they're totally gone?" Huda asked. "Before all those landmarks downtown change?"

Dina stayed frozen in her place and looked defiantly at her mother. "I didn't even know what they were like before! Why would I care?"

Huda hadn't thought of that. How could she have forgotten that Dina was born and raised during the war? That what Dina's generation knew of Beirut was different from what her generation had known? Yesterday in the Burj Square she had seen, in the middle of the rubble, the jewelry market with bracelets and necklaces shining through the shop windows. As she had headed toward Dabbas Square, she had recalled the names of the movies she had seen at the Roxy and Dunia cinemas. And when she had gone up to Bab-Idrees and stood in front of the entrance to the al-Tawila marketplace—now blocked by piles of stones—she had seen the last sweater she'd bought there as a present for her mother. Her memory penetrated the charred walls of the burned-out café, the Pâtisserie Suisse, where they used to gorge themselves with ice cream and cake on Saturday evenings. Was she drawn downtown because it was associated with the most beautiful memories of her past? Or because both the downtown and her past were wiped out at the same time?

"You didn't know my Beirut, Dina," she explained. "Just think of it as a visit to the ruins of a modern city, just like we visit the ruins of ancient cities—Ba'albeck, Byblos, Sidon, and Tyre."

"But we like to see those cities because we study them in history class."

Her daughter's answer was immediate, and Huda quickly grabbed the opportunity to retaliate. "Beirut still has ancient ruins, even though most of them are gone."

Dina persisted, "So there's no point in visiting the memory of them."

Huda couldn't help but laugh. "Not just the memory of them, Dina," she said. "Some of them are still standing there. You'll see."

They had finished washing and drying the dishes. Huda noticed the disappointment on her daughter's face as she put her jacket on, but she ignored it, and they left together.

They got out of the cab and walked toward the Burj Square.

"Mom, why do they call it the Burj Square?" Dina asked, finally showing some interest.

"Because a tower had been built there, on the edge of the square, to watch for enemies attacking from the land," Huda explained. She pointed toward the southwest corner of the square: "The tower disappeared more than a hundred years ago. In that same area, an Italian architect built Prince Fakhr al-Din a beautiful palace with a huge marble pool in the front. The palace was surrounded by gardens filled with statues. Unfortunately, nothing's left of those masterpieces. Even the small castle the Ottomans built there," she pointed in the opposite direction, "even that castle, which remained standing until the first half of this century, is gone without a trace."

They stood in silence, contemplating the burned-out buildings and piles of rubble. Then, thinking out loud, Huda said, "Oddly enough, collective memory has kept the name of a tower that protected Beirut from its enemies while the other masterpieces are forgotten: the palace, the pool, the gardens, the statues." She continued, "I wonder if it's because traces of war stick in our heads more than those of peace? Or maybe the memory chooses from the past what it wants to keep, what it wishes weren't gone?"

Dina didn't comment on her mother's reflections, and they walked slowly down the street that had given up its asphalt for mud puddles, stones, and wild plants. They had to watch where they were going, and then Huda stopped again to explain some things to Dina.

"On that corner was the famous Li'zaz Café. Dad told me he used to go there when he was a teenager to listen to the storyteller tell the epic of 'Antara and other popular tales."

"What about Grandma?"

Huda laughed. "It wasn't common for women to go to such cafés back then."

"That would suck," Dina said.

"It did. Next to that famous café, there was a jewelry market as well as a popular movie theater called Cristal. Farther down, all that's left are the marquees, the Opéra and the Rêve au Lit. In the '50s, Dina, the movie theaters in the al-Hamra, Kaslik, and Jounieh areas weren't built yet. So when we were kids, we used to go to the movies here."

When they reached the middle of the square, Huda pointed to a heap of rubble on her right. "There used to be a police station over there. Too bad it was demolished. It was one of the most beautiful buildings left from the Ottoman period."

"You miss the Ottoman period when we're standing in front of the statues for the martyrs the Ottomans hanged?"

Huda was upset by her daughter's comment. "I don't miss those times," she explained. "I miss the architectural masterpieces that were built during the Ottoman period. Besides, it wasn't the tyrants who created those masterpieces, Dina. It was the people, the architects, the laborers, and the craftsmen. They were victims, too."

Why had she mentioned only the police station and not Marika's House, right behind it? Was it because she didn't want to bring up prostitution to her daughter or because she didn't want to dwell on the news she'd been reading in the papers every day or on the image of little Sana from yesterday?

Dina was contemplating the martyrs' statue, now riddled by the bullets of people trying to make more martyrs. The woman still stood there, holding up the torch of liberty, her hand on the shoulder of a young man. Two other young men were at her feet, one in front of her and the other behind her. All of them were looking up.

"You think they're looking up at the future, Mom?"

"Will the future remember its martyrs?" Huda wondered instead of answering her daughter and led her toward some chairs lined up by the statue's base. A few were shaded by umbrellas with Marlboro ads. Another sign stood by the umbrellas: "The Martyrs' Café."

This is the present's way of mocking its martyrs, Huda thought bitterly.

"Some pictures of the old tower, ma'am?" a street vendor said, displaying a collection of cheap, colorful postcards. Huda declined and asked the owner of the café for two cold sodas.

━━ ━━ I knew him, but I didn't ever really know him. I knew he was always late for the first class. I would have started by telling how the Shehabis took over the Ma'anis and how the Ottoman pasha of Sidon suddenly withdrew after receiving the news of Prince Haydar al-Shehabi's victory in the battle of 'Ayn-Dara. I would go into details about the historical events I wanted them to learn *from*—not just learn—to gain something that might enlighten their futures, something that would shed light on the differences between our past and present, and guide them toward their future. I could sense the enthusiasm in my voice every time I pointed out that Prince Haydar al-Shehabi, who was a Muslim, was also the prince of the Druze and the protector of the Christian patriarch, whom the Ottomans were trying to capture. As usual, the door would open slowly. I would see him from the corner of my eye, tiptoeing, sneaking to a seat in the back of the classroom. I would tense up and lose my enthusiasm, and I would stop talking. I would stare at him until he sat down, and with my eyes on him, everybody's eyes would fix on him. His lowered head and the blush on his face were proof of his embarrassment, something I hoped would keep him from being late again, but no. . . .

"If you keep coming late, Ahmad, I'll have to ask you not to attend class anymore," I said once. But he kept arriving late, and I ran out of patience.

"Do you want me to expel you?" I asked. "Do you ever think about how much money your father's paying for your education?"

"Yes, I do," he said. "I come every day from my village in the South."

"Then maybe you should leave the house half an hour earlier if you want to be here on time."

Then Ahmad disappeared. A day, two days, a whole week passed. I started wondering if he wasn't able to make it to class on time and had decided to give up on my lectures. I felt guilty. To silence my conscience, I kept telling myself he must be sick. Then I asked his friends about him. When they said they hadn't seen him, I concluded that he really was sick.

One day I came to class and started my lecture, "In 1822, Naser Abdullah, the pasha of Sidon, Prince Bashir . . . ," when my eyes fell on Ahmad, who was, as usual, seated in the back of the classroom, except this time he had arrived before me. The paleness of his face confirmed my assumptions: he *was* sick, and my reprimanding him had actually worked. I experienced the glory of victory and the rewards of being strict with my students—for their own good. I told myself it was our negligence in this country that had gotten us where we were and that we were now reaping the results of such negligence. My confidence in myself and my educational methods increased.

Ahmad never came in late after that. He was always there before me, but he was pale and thin, and a hint of sadness never left his face. Was I imagining that?

"Are you sick, Ahmad?" I asked him after class. I didn't want him to mistake my strictness for harshness and inconsideration. He didn't answer, so I asked again.

"No, not at all."

"I thought maybe you were sick because you look so pale and thin . . . because you've been absent for a while." He walked away without saying anything.

A week later I was waiting for the university mail room to open. The employee arrived and unlocked the door, and when he opened it, somebody came out. Ahmad! How had he gotten in when the room was locked? He hurried away without acknowledging me.

Abu Ishaq told me that about two months earlier, when he was locking up the mail room, he had seen a figure disappear behind the mailboxes. He wanted to chase him, but he got nervous. If it was a thief, he thought, he'd definitely be armed. Only a thief could hide there. Abu Ishaq had a wife and children, so he was afraid that if he was killed, no one would take care of his family. Besides, what could anyone steal from the mail room anyway? Abu Ishaq was certain that the thief didn't know that the room was just the mail room, so he had gone out of the room, locked the door, and left.

"After dinner, I told Umm Ishaq about the stupid thief who was going to find himself locked in a room with nothing to steal . . . " Abu Ishaq explained. "Then I remembered: the stamps! There were hundreds of stamps in the drawer, and I was in charge of them. How could I have forgotten? I swear on my children's life, ma'am, I couldn't sleep all night. I couldn't wait for daylight to come. I put on my clothes and hurried to the university. I didn't even drink the coffee Umm Ishaq had fixed for me."

"Weren't you afraid of the robber anymore?"

"I could only think of the stamps. I was afraid the administration would accuse me of stealing them, that they would fire me, and I'd lose my only source of income. I asked the night guard to come with me since he was armed. I put the key in silently and opened the door a crack. I didn't see anybody. We tiptoed inside, and I headed toward the drawer. I checked it and told the guard it was still locked, and then I took the key out of my pocket to open it. My hands were shaking so much I dropped the key. When I bent to pick it up, I glimpsed a pair of legs running outside. 'Stop, thief!' I yelled, but he disappeared before the guard could follow him."

"So you couldn't tell who it was?'

Abu Ishaq ignored my question. He told me that he counted the stamps and nothing was missing. Then he searched the room and found a pile of folded newspapers with a blanket on top and a bundle of clothes next to it in the corner behind the boxes.

"Naturally, I informed the school administration of what had happened. They asked me to watch the room so we could find out whose belongings they were and why he slept there. I wasn't afraid anymore. I waited there until the evening, and when I saw the same figure disappear behind the mailboxes, I followed him."

"Was it Ahmad?" I asked, amazed.

"I asked him who he was and why he had been sleeping here. He told me he was a student and that his name was—yes—Ahmad, but he refused to tell me why he slept there. I asked him to inform the school administration."

"He's been sleeping here for two months, and you still don't know why?"

"Yes, two months, and I don't know *exactly* why. His friends told me that he'd left his village and that he didn't have a house in Beirut. He doesn't have any money either. That must be why he sleeps here."

It had never occurred to me that my insistence on punctuality would come to that. Embarrassment and guilt replaced my feelings of victory and self-confidence.

"I'd like to see you in my office after class, Ahmad," I said.

"She's been picking on me since the beginning of the semester," I overheard him telling Elias. "What does she want from me now?"

I ignored what he said and went to wait for him in my office. I told myself that I had the right to be strict because punctuality was a university regulation—and a mark of good manners.

"Yes, Doctor?"

I didn't miss the defiance in his voice or the bold expression on his face when I looked up at him. Would I have been any nicer if I had been the one spending my nights in a mail room—especially to the person who had caused it?

"Have a seat, Ahmad," I said, pointing to a seat in front of my desk. He sat down, and we were silent for a minute. Then I said, "I'm sorry, Ahmad, if I'm the reason why you left your village and are sleeping on the mail-room floor. It didn't occur to me . . ."

"It has nothing to do with you," he interrupted me.

"Go home, Ahmad," I continued, apologetically. "I won't penalize you for being late. Anyway, the semester is almost over, and it's really not worth it."

"Thank you," he said and left. But he kept arriving at class before me and sleeping in the mail room, from what Abu Ishaq told me. Was it because the semester was almost over, and it wasn't "worth it"? Was he punishing me for being strict? Making me feel guilty? So be it. I had my own problems to deal with, so I also dropped the whole issue.

It was Friday, the last day of school. The next week was final exams week. Just before the end of class, we felt the classroom shake. An Israeli raid: we could hear the airplanes. In a moment, the class was empty, and I hurried to my office.

"Israeli airplanes have attacked the Cité Sportive and the surrounding Palestinian refugee camps," the announcer was saying when we turned on the transistor radios that never left our sides in those days. All I could think of was Dina. I picked up my bag and ran all the way to her school. Lots of cars were parked in front of the gate, one row next to the other, blocking the road. The honking grew louder. People were swearing and yelling.

"How on earth did they get here that fast?" I wondered as I hurried among them, walking—thank God. The school hallway was full of parents waiting for their children.

"There are lots of casualties, according to the news."

"The walls and foundations of Cité Sportive are all cracked."

"Not just the Cité Sportive, the houses around it, too."

"I don't think so; Israel knows where to strike. Most of the time, all they hit is the camps."

"What about the people? People are in those camps. What about the people on the streets?"

I listened to the other parents' news, their comments. Finally somebody brought Dina to me. I pulled her close to me. I kissed her, and we left.

"We heard the planes, Mom," she said. "Where were they?"

"Far from our house, dear. Don't worry."

"What about Dad?"

"He leaves the office early on Fridays," I explained. "Don't worry about him. We'll call Grandma and find out."

I went into the kitchen to prepare the salad and warm the food. Dina rushed to the phone, and I heard her ask about him, but I couldn't tell what answers she was getting.

"Grandma says Dad isn't home yet."

"I'm sure it's the traffic," I reassured her and myself.

"She'll tell him to call when he gets there."

I stopped gazing at the cucumber I was chopping and scrutinized her face, her eyes. It seemed to me that my explanation had reassured her and that she wasn't worried anymore. Was that the innocence of childhood?

"Set the table, Dina."

What if something happened to him? I wondered to myself. I don't think so. My heart is my guide. I had to laugh at myself. If it had been my guide, it would have told me what was going to happen before it actually happened. Perhaps I didn't have a heart, as he was always saying—and as Ahmad, among other students, no doubt would have said. I carried the food to the table, and we ate in silence.

"You think Dad's back yet?"

The innocence of childhood? *My* ignorance, *my* innocence. I cursed the war for the thousandth time. I thought of the worries of children all over the world. Or did only our children have them? I remembered things I'd read about Cambodia, Biafra, and Vietnam. Was power worth all that struggle? Did it justify all that blood, the blood of the innocent?

"You think Dad's back yet?" Dina repeated.

"He would've called," I said. "Something must've held him up. Don't worry, dear. The raid was in a distant neighborhood," I reassured her, trying also to reassure myself, but in vain. Her questions brought back my misgivings. The raid was far from us; it wasn't far from the houses near the Cité Sportive. Had he been going there? Or coming from there? I stood up and went into the kitchen to do the dishes. Dina picked up the towel and starting drying without my asking her to, without the usual begging and pleading. That wasn't like her.

"Mom, how do children live in countries where there isn't any war?" she asked. She was worried because her father wasn't back yet.

"Same as you. They eat, sleep, play, and go to school."

"Every day?"

"Every day."

"You think their bomb shelters are like ours?"

I laughed. "They don't need them, Dina," I explained. "There's no war there."

"You mean they never get scared?"

"Of course they do," I said. "Not of bombs or missiles, but of speeding cars, drunks on the street, mean dogs."

She was quiet, and then she said, "They can always watch out for cars and drunks and dogs. We—"

"Us too. We can avoid missiles and bombs by staying in the shelter."

"What if we're on the street?"

Was she asking that because her father might be on the street? I snapped, "God protects us."

"Then why didn't He protect all those people who got killed?"

Her logic was too much for me.

"Why didn't He protect all those who got killed?"

"We don't know God's will, Dina," I said. "Thanks for the dishes. Go to your room and start your homework."

"Tomorrow's Saturday, Mom," she said. "I don't have school. You think God will protect Dad?"

The sound of the phone saved me. Dina ran and picked up the receiver.

"Dad, thank God you called." Once I knew he was safe, I didn't listen to the rest of their conversation.

On Monday, the schools announced that they were going to be closed, so I left Dina at my neighbors' house and went to the university. I met with the dean, who insisted that it was impossible for us to proceed with the final exams as long as Israel was invading Lebanon. I left him and joined the few students on campus; Ahmad was among them.

"Any news from your village, Ahmad?" I asked. "Have you been able to check on your family?"

He turned and walked away. Was he that resentful? The thought made me furious, and I looked at the others.

"What's the matter with him?" I asked. "Why is he acting like that? Is it because I reprimanded him for being late? Isn't—"

I stopped. They looked baffled. "You don't know?" Suhail asked.

"Know what?"

"What happened."

"To whom?"

"To his family, his home."

"His family?" I didn't understand.

"Two months ago I went home with Ahmad," he explained. "We got out of a cab at the crossroad and walked until we entered the village. 'Strange,' Ahmad said, 'we haven't run into anybody yet.' That's when I heard the silence. It was deafening. We walked faster. 'Even the gas station is closed,' he said as we hurried along. 'There must have been an Israeli raid. We're used to them,' he said calmly. I wondered if he was trying to reassure me."

"Was it really a raid?" I asked.

Suhail kept talking, "We walked even faster. I could tell it was because he was worried. There was no way they could've gotten used to raids. Ahmad suddenly stopped in front of a huge pile of rubble . . . stones and metal and broken wood. Next to the rubble was another house that had been transformed into a pile of stones. 'My home!' Ahmad yelled. Then he started shaking and didn't take another step."

So that explained all the mystery: why he started getting to class before me, why he slept in the mail room.

"What about his parents?" I asked.

Again, Suhail didn't answer. He continued, "I squeezed his arm and said, 'The most important thing right now is for your family to be okay.' But, Doctor, I was really afraid. I was terrified. We started running. Ahmad headed for the closest house. 'They've been bombing the resistance offices, the training centers. But now our houses?' he said while we ran. We had almost reached that house when we started hearing unintelligible noises. The noises suddenly stopped when the people saw us at the door. The room was full of men who turned to look at Ahmad. He froze at the porch, searching for his father and brothers among those men. I read those faces: sadness, anger, resentment, despair. 'Where's my father?' Ahmad yelled. 'And As'ad and Hasan?'"

"Weren't they in the room?"

Suhail ignored my question and kept talking. "A tall, heavy-set guy came up to us, but before he could say anything, a woman came out of the living room. She suddenly started wailing, and her wailing was followed by yelling and sobbing from the living room. Ahmad ran toward her, but two men grabbed him. 'Let go of me,' he yelled. 'I want my mother, Samia.' But the woman wasn't his mother. Then all of a sudden the wailing stopped."

"What happened?"

"Basically what happened was that his parents were in the field when the raid took them by surprise. They all got killed, and their house was destroyed along with other village houses."

Suhail didn't say any more. I had never felt as guilty and embarrassed as I did at that moment. "You're not the reason for my leaving my village," he had told me, but I was the one who had humiliated him, who had threatened him. I had refused to ignore minor, absurd regulations at a time when absurdity was taking over our existence.

I asked (because asking about details—wanting to know them—confirms the guilt and absolves it to a certain extent), "Did you go to the burial with him? The collective burial?"

Amer answered for him, "They had already buried them before Ahmad and Suhail got there." I completely understood why.

Suhail added, "Ahmad was angry when they told him that. He protested and cried. I tried to calm him down. 'It's better this way, Ahmad,' I had said. 'You'll remember them talking and laughing and working, exactly as you knew them the way they were, and that's what will remain with you, instead of the image of them—'"

Suhail choked on the word, even after all these months.

"You were right, Suhail," I said. "It's better that he didn't see them before they were buried."

The mail room had become Ahmad's home, and he a refugee—one of the hundreds of thousands who had become refugees in their own country.

⸺ ⸺ Sitting by the base of the statue in the Burj Square, Huda thought to herself, we haven't celebrated Martyrs' Day in years. She looked at her daughter, sitting across from her—her sixteen-year-old daughter was only six the last time they celebrated it. Dina was still with her that day. And now? At least she's alive, *alive,* Huda repeated to herself and took a sip of her soda.

⁓ ⁓ June, July, August. Two days after the raid on al-Madinah al-Riyadiyah, the Israelis entered the South with an unprecedented number of soldiers, tanks, and trucks. They bombed Tyre, Sidon, and al-Miya Miya. We unfolded the map of Lebanon and followed the enemy's advance, hour after hour. Where did the forty kilometers of their so-called safety belt end? It became clear that an Israeli kilometer was different from the standard kilometer. The village al-Damour fell. Military airplanes and battleships bombed the suburbs of Beirut first and then the city itself.

I tried to entertain Dina. We played games with the neighbors' children in the bomb shelter: dominoes, checkers, and Snakes and Ladders. When the raids subsided, I would read her stories: *The Deer Hunter*, *Uncle Tom's Cabin*, *Umm Mahfouz's Box*, and *Baba Mabrouk*. Between playing games and reading stories, I'd follow the news of the outside world: a building was demolished in the al-Ramleh al-Bayda'. A new bomb—the fusion bomb—went off in a building in the al-Sanaye', wiping it out along with the scores of families who were in it. The announcers warned children not to touch tiny balls they might find in streets and parks because those balls might have been parts of fission bombs. I smiled at fate's way of mocking us: the terms *fission* and *fusion* enriched our language while the bombs themselves obliterated our existence! Then I ran out of ideas for entertaining Dina.

The Israelis were besieging Beirut. They cut the water and power, and it became hard to get vegetables, fruit, and meat into the city. It also became hard for Sharif to keep in touch with us every day and to check on Dina because the phone lines were cut off. Some buildings had wells and electric generators, so I would stand in line in front of them—along with Dina and scores of other women, men, and children. We'd fill our plastic containers with water and then carry our precious load back home. We stored some of the water in the bathtub and the rest in glass bottles, which we sterilized in the sun for two hours as a specialist from the American University Hospital had recommended.

Sometimes we'd go to the supermarket, looking for a can of peas that others might have missed or a can of corn beef hidden in the corner of a shelf. Everything disappeared from the shelves: macaroni, bulgur wheat, lentils, chickpeas, rice, sugar, and canned food.

Well, not all the canned food disappeared. There was one shelf still full. A woman attacked the shelf and started shoving cans in her bag.

"You're worried about feeding your dogs and cats?" I couldn't help but ask her.

She didn't stop filling her bag, but she glared at me. "Those are for me and my children."

Could they have been that hungry? Then it occurred to me that perhaps she couldn't read English and thought that the dogs and cats on the cans were the company's logo.

"Ma'am, this food is for pets," I said.

She looked up at me, still holding the can. Was I making fun of her? Lying to her?

"For pets?" she asked, "When people can't find anything to eat? That's insane." Thinking that I was trying to beat her to the cans, she put more of them in her bag.

I smiled and said calmly, "If they were for people, ma'am, you wouldn't have found them here by now."

She took her hand off the can she was about to grab. Did my logic convince her? She lowered her head, contemplating the contents of her bag. Was she trying to hide her disappointment? Her regret that her children weren't cats or dogs? A few minutes later she raised her head and slowly started returning the cans to where they belonged. I noticed a repressed tear and quickly walked away.

Between carrying water and looking for food, we listened to the transistor radio, informing us of the negotiations between the Lebanese government and Philip Habib, the U.S. special envoy, as well as between the prime minister and the Palestine Liberation Organization. Our hopes for resolutions would rise one day ("Is Dad coming home?" Dina would ask), only to be shattered the next day. Finally an agreement was reached. The Palestinian fighters would leave Beirut under the supervision and protection of a multinational force. A new president would be elected, and for two or three weeks we breathed a sigh of relief.

"Mom, Mom," Dina said, "Dad's here!"

I was doing laundry that had been piling up for months. Dina saw him from the window and ran to open the door. She hurried down the stairs to meet him. She had finally gotten used to things, even though they still didn't make sense to her.

"Rima's dad lives with them. Hanan's dad lives with them. Nabil's dad lives with them. Why doesn't my dad live with us? " she'd ask. "He doesn't love me?"

"Of course he loves you."

"Then he doesn't love *you*."

I said nothing.

"Why did you get married?"

"Because we loved each other," I answered without thinking.

"So why did he leave you?"

I would change the subject. The adults never understood. Why would she? Sharif came in, carrying Dina.

"You're not a baby anymore, Dina," I said. "You're seven years old."

"Dad's carrying me because he misses me."

Why did I always have to be so strict? I thought of Ahmad.

"I'm taking her swimming today," he said, putting her down. "It's been months."

"Please say yes, Mom," Dina said. "Please say yes."

"Yes, of course."

At five in the evening, I turned on the transistor radio to listen to the news—out of habit, not because I was expecting any surprises. But there had been a surprise: the headquarters of the Phalange Party—where the newly elected president and his assistants were—had been blown up. The president miraculously survived.

But a few minutes later: no, he didn't survive. He was transported to the hospital in an ambulance.

There was a loud knock on my door.

"Huda, have you heard the news?"

My neighbors were bewildered, too, not so much by that piece of news as much as by the fear of returning to the vicious circle of violence, the fear of shelling and death and destruction—the fear of the unknown tomorrow. We kept our ears fixed to the transistor radio as we turned the dial from one station to another. At nine, the accurate information was broadcast: the elected president had lost his life, along with the rest of the participants at the conference. Who assassinated him? Why was he assassinated? More important, what was waiting for us tomorrow?

We got the answer to that question before the dawn broke. A strange roar pulled me out of my restless sleep. I pointed the flashlight at my watch; it was 3:00 A.M. I went to the window: orange beams shone under the full moon. They were advancing slowly. I couldn't take my eyes off the tanks and trucks. The Israelis had entered Beirut!

I waited for two days, and—once again—I had to leave Dina at my neighbors' house to go to the university.

"What's the point?" my neighbor tried to dissuade me. "The administration can't make any decisions as long as we don't know what'll happen."

"Or do you just want to look at the Israelis in our streets?" her husband added. I ignored him (as usual he wanted to insult me, the woman abandoned by her husband).

"I want to check on my colleagues and students."

It was ten in the morning. The streets were almost deserted. A few pedestrians were walking with their heads held low. Out of fear? Humiliation? Despair? They were walking, as I was, along the walls—almost glued to them. Not one smiled.

I saw a small group of people in one corner of the courtyard. I recognized Elias, Zeina, Layla, and Suhail. I went up to them. They told me that none of them had been hurt and that only the dean and Dr. Halim Nasser had come. They had no sooner mentioned Halim than he walked up and joined us.

"What about Ahmad? Have you seen him?"

"Oh yeah, Ahmad's been sleeping here," Zeina said. Then she looked down the street and burst out laughing. "You should've asked for a million dollars."

We saw Ahmad coming from a distance.

"Does anybody want a *man'ousheh?*" he asked. "I'm going to the bakery."

As soon as he passed through the gate, we heard a whistle and someone yell, "Stop!" We froze for a second, then ran toward the street. At the curve, to the left, were four Israeli soldiers. Who were they talking to? Who were they giving orders to? The street was empty except for Ahmad. We saw him stop for a minute and then take off running, running.

"He's insane," Layla said. Our eyes stayed fixed on his back as it moved farther and farther away. "Why doesn't he stop?"

A whistling bullet came as answer, followed by the hissing of two more. His body swayed, took two more steps before dropping to the ground.

"Oh!" I muffled Layla's scream with my hands.

"Hush, Layla," I said. "We don't need another victim."

We saw the soldiers run toward the body.

"Why did they kill him?" Zeina's whispered question didn't conceal the anger in her voice.

"Because he didn't stop," Halim said.

"Why didn't he stop?"

"He doesn't have an ID, remember?" Suhail replied. "What would he tell the Israelis? That they destroyed his house? Burned his documents? Murdered his family?"

I thought to myself: a civilization that acknowledges nothing but documents. Documents don't exist for the sake of people. They're the evidence that people exist . . . and their nonexistence causes people's nonexistence.

"This way he's given them a reason to accuse him—just like they accuse us all—of being a terrorist," Elias said. "They destroy 'only the houses of terrorists,' isn't that what they claim? That they kill only terrorists?"

The four soldiers had reached Ahmad. One of them straightened his legs and turned him over with his boots. Like statues, we stood watching the scene from behind the fence. We saw the back of the blue shirt turn dark red before touching the ground. The buildings and trees whirled around me. I held onto the wall and shut my eyes. When I opened them, I saw an Israeli soldier leaning over Ahmad, looking through one pocket and then the other. He took out some bills, nothing else. He put them into his pocket, looked at his friends, and said something. They smiled. One of them kicked the body, and then they left. I felt dizzy again. My breakfast rose from my stomach, and I ran to a corner, leaned on a tree, and threw up. I threw up everything, even the bile from the center of my being. Tears of rage. I felt Halim stand beside me. He handed me a wad of tissues.

Behind me, I heard Suhail saying, "They're gone. Let's go to Ahmad."

"I can't," Zeina and Layla said at the same time. I stayed with them.

Two days later I saw Ahmad's worn blanket flung on top of a pile of trash on the curb.

━━ ━━ "We haven't celebrated Martyrs' Day for years," Huda repeated, contemplating the holes in the bodies of the statues in front of her and in the arm holding up the torch of freedom. Freedom?

Seeing her mother had finished her soda, Dina asked, "You're ready? Let's go home. I'm sick of this depressing place. The Burj Square should be called—"

"The Martyrs' Square," Huda continued. "I think that's the best name for it right now"—even though they had forgotten the Martyrs' Day during the war, she thought to herself. Why have they forgotten it? Was it because the martyrs back then were different from our martyrs? But then there were only fourteen martyrs, whereas we have hundreds of thousands. Was it because those martyrs sacrificed themselves, but ours were sacrificed by other people? Then she remembered that only the fourteen people who were hanged were known. What about the thousands who died of starvation afterwards? Even the collective graves where their bodies lay were no longer known. Hundreds of corpses had been collected each day in government carts. They were the corpses of people whose fathers, mothers, children, brothers, and sisters mourned their death, just as we mourn the deaths of ours. History doesn't remember their names, just as it won't remember the names of our martyrs. Were our martyrs the only ones sacrificed by other people? What about them? Weren't they victims of Jamal Pasha and the opportunistic dealers of wheat? Why then have people forgotten Martyrs' Day?

She and Dina hailed a cab, her questions still unanswered.

— 3 —

SHARIF AL-MUKHTAR PARKED HIS CAR and turned off the engine. He opened the door for his companion, and they got out. Sharif walked slowly, and the other man followed him. Then they stood contemplating the view before them. Neither one said anything.

⁓ ⁓ "Why don't you quit your job with the government, Sharif? Find a new job? Become a freelancer?"

"Nobody wants to hire someone who's spent so many years working for the government," I would tell Huda.

"But they know you. They know you're an honest lawyer with great potential."

"That's the problem," I'd answer, exasperated. "They want a lawyer who'll manipulate the law to their advantage, mostly against the country's interests, against my conscience."

"But the respectable companies, the banks, need to consult an honest lawyer, someone they can trust. Someone with your loyalty and qualifications."

"You think they need me?" I laughed. "No, my dear. They can always consult their relatives, friends, and acquaintances, people from their own class. I'm a nobody in those circles."

Was she starting to look down on my job, now that she was on her way to becoming a college professor? Did she feel she deserved more than a simple government employee? I'd stop talking, and the shelling would start up again, so she'd stop, too. I'd stay at home—or in the bomb shelter—for days, for weeks. I'd read the paper, listen to the news, play backgammon with Tawfiq or Salah and dominos or Snakes and Ladders with Dina, or read a book.

Huda was always immersed in her books, her research. I couldn't talk to her, didn't dare interrupt her. What would I say anyway? That I was bored? She knew that but didn't care. All she cared about was herself—her plans and her future. Even Dina became my responsibility because her mother was too busy, whereas I had nothing to do.

I was useless.

The battles would subside, and I'd go to the office. There'd be only three or four of us. We'd comment on the news and give updates to those who hadn't heard. One hour. A couple of hours. Then we'd all go home. Eventually I was the only one who still showed up for work—until I gave up too. I watched Huda read, write, and do housework while I sat reading the paper or listening to the news. The paper seemed like an exact copy of the days before, repeating news of shelling, killing, and destruction in the same neighborhoods. I would doze off while listening to the news and then fall into a deep sleep.

"Why don't you go get us some vegetables, fruit, and meat, Sharif?"

I'd go to the store at the end of the street. Although it wasn't on her list, I would buy Dina a chocolate bar and then come home to my chair in the corner where I'd doze off and go to sleep.

"How can you sleep with what's happening around you, with what's happening to our friends, for that matter?" she once yelled. "Anis hasn't come home. He's been gone for two days. Tamima's been running around from one militia to another, from one organization to another, asking questions, pleading, weeping, offering a reward, but she hasn't learned a thing."

I looked at Huda. I was worried about Anis. Although I ached for Tamima's plight, I was helpless. Helpless. Was I the only one? I shut my eyes again so I didn't have to see her anger, her contempt. Her studies, dissertation, and degree kept her busy. Didn't she have a heart? What about me? I slept.

A few days later she exploded: "You don't even care about what might happen to us. If I'd been standing in line at the bakery, that bomb would have killed me too."

"Well, I would have been killed by that car bomb if I'd been at the market buying you fruit and vegetables."

What was the point of thinking of everything that might have happened to her, to Dina, to me, to our friends? I didn't want to hear the sound of the shelling or think about danger and death because I couldn't do anything about them, so I slept. I slept, and everything around me vanished. I would forget that Huda and Dina might die, just as other women and children were dying every day . . . women and children. I drugged myself with sleep. Consciously or unconsciously.

"Dr. As'ad and his family are leaving for Paris so his children can finally have a normal school year," she told me one day.

"So your royal highness wants to go to Paris?" I asked. "Great, as long as your salary is enough. Me, I'm a simple employee. I'm not a doctor like As'ad."

"That's not what I meant," she said. "I was just wondering where we'd take Dina in case she got sick."

"The country's not out of doctors yet," I said. "We'll find someone else."

"It's out of good doctors. They're gone!" She was quiet for a moment. Then she said, "Not just the doctors."

"I'm not as successful as those people. You should have known that from the beginning. Am I not good enough for you anymore?"

My gaze fell on Dina, frozen at her bedroom door. Tears were in her eyes. She looked worried. Children pay for the sins of their fathers. Was Dina paying for mine? I swallowed my anger, went back to my seat, and shut my eyes.

Two days later there was a knock at the door. It was our neighbor Salah. He had come to play backgammon.

"Tell Wafa' not to make dinner," I told him, looking at Huda from the corner of my eye. "You and the children are having dinner with us tonight."

Huda looked up from the papers in front of her, turned her head halfway, and then went back to her papers without saying a word. Her papers could go to hell! Didn't I have the right to have people over to my house? Didn't I have a wife who did what she was supposed to do?

Salah left to tell his wife, and I said to Huda, "Do you have anything to fix for dinner, or should I go to the store before it closes?" Then I set up the backgammon.

"Can't you see I'm busy?" she said. "Did you have to invite them?"

"I didn't have to. I wanted to. For once I want to feel as if I have a house where I can have people over and a wife who does what she's supposed to do. No one ever visits us, and we visit no one. I'm sick of this life."

She gave me a list of the things she needed, and I went to the store. Our neighbors showed up at eight on the dot.

"What would you like to drink?" Huda asked.

"You worry about the food," I told her before Salah or Wafa' could answer. She disappeared into the kitchen without saying a word.

I was still the one in charge—I proved this to Salah and Wafa'. I handed the kids some sodas and fixed tumblers of whiskey for Wafa', Salah, and myself.

"I'll have mine in the kitchen with Huda," Wafa' said, carrying her drink to the other room. I don't know what they talked about. Huda was silent at dinner, and I was left to entertain our guests, to make sure they felt welcome. The children's laughter lightened the atmosphere. Still, I couldn't help saying, "You'll have to excuse Huda. It's been so long since we've had people over that she's almost forgotten how to make conversation. The only people she talks to are her students." Then I changed the subject right away and started commenting on the news I read that day. It was the last time I invited anybody over.

Finally, the fighting stopped. Again I started going to the office. Again I was alone. Years of futile work . . . and now what? No work at all. Dina's worried face haunted me. Was it reproach I read in her eyes or confusion? Was she, too, beginning to lose respect for me? Was she comparing me, her failure of a father, to her busy mother? This idea upset me even more than Huda's anger, more than the sounds of bombs, and more than even death itself.

At last I made up my mind.

⸺ ⸺ "Is that the place, Mr. al-Mukhtar?" The man's voice brought him back to the present.

Sharif was silent for a moment, then he said, "Yes, that's it."

⸺ ⸺ I didn't want to call from home. I went to the office because I knew no one would be there.

"Hello, I'd like to speak to Mr. Jawad, please."

"May I ask who's calling?" the secretary asked softly, trying to determine who it was before letting me know if Jawad was there.

"Sharif al-Mukhtar, an old friend."

"One moment please. Let me see if he's around," she said, as I'd expected.

A moment later Jawad was on the phone, "Hi, Sharif. What a nice surprise! How are you doing? How's Huda? And Dina?"

His enthusiasm and warm voice encouraged me to go on.

"Fine, Jawad," I said. "I'm actually calling because I need to see you . . . it's personal."

"When?"

"Whenever you like," I said. "You're the busy one, not me."

Did he notice the bitterness in my voice? I waited for a moment before he said, "How about Thursday afternoon? Why don't I come over to your house? That way I can also see Huda and Dina."

"No, Jawad," I said. "I'll stop by your office. It's between the two of us."

I heard him hesitate and imagined the surprised look on his face. He said, "Okay, whatever you want. Three, then."

The days leading up to Thursday were full of anticipation, the nights full of anxiety. I didn't mention anything to Huda. Jawad might refuse, so nobody else needed to know. What if he accepted? I was haunted by fears of the terms he might demand if he did agree. It was a business I knew nothing about. I was afraid it wouldn't work out because I didn't know anything about the business and the country's situation hadn't stabilized. On top of all those fears was my terror of debt. I had never borrowed a dime in my life. And now? But success was guaranteed. And profit too. And relief from the depression of my futile job. I had studied the market. Demand was rising despite the war. Imported products were expensive, so there was a demand for local products. But would I be able to pay off my debt? If so, when? In the end, I wasn't sure I really wanted him to say yes . . . until Thursday finally came.

He opened the door for me this time. "Hello, come on in."

After crossing the empty reception room, I walked ahead of him to his office without saying anything.

"Have a seat, Sharif," he said. "Too bad everyone's already gone. There's no one to make us coffee."

"Thanks, that's all right." I looked around the fancy office—the bookshelves behind his desk, the walls covered with delicate wallpaper and decorated with two watercolors by Omar Unsi and an oil painting by an artist whose name I couldn't decipher.

"Here," he said, extending a box of chocolate in front of me. "Instead of the coffee." I glimpsed the word *Lindt* on the wrapper. Of course he could afford the best chocolate. In an attempt to stay calm, I took one and started unwrapping it to soften my fears, though it would have been better for me to cut to the chase and put an end to my anxiety, my doubts.

"So, Sharif," he said. "What's the problem? You've got me worried." It was as if he had read my mind.

"Listen, Jawad, I've decided to quit my job." I examined his face. He raised his eyebrows, and I read his question before he even asked.

"Now? With everything that's going on?"

Was that concern in his eyes or exasperation? Fear that I might ask him for help? But I was already there, so no turning back.

"My salary isn't enough anymore."

"What about Huda's?"

"It's barely anything," I said. "Besides, she spends it all on her university expenses, books, and clothes she didn't need before she went back to school."

"What are you going to do? Have you seriously thought about it?"

I mustered up courage, "That's why I'm here for advice . . . to ask for your help."

Now his eyes were cautious, and his face was filled with . . . hesitation? Maybe it was all in my head. He didn't say anything.

"I inherited a piece of land from my father," I continued. "It's away from the battle zones. I've been thinking of building a small factory there to make—"

"A factory?" he interrupted.

"To make zippers," I said, blocking out his surprise, reservation, and disapproval. "A small factory won't cost more than thirty or forty thousand dollars. People have to wear something and imported clothes are expensive, so there's been more demand for clothes that are locally produced. I studied the market. I know a venture like this can't fail."

"Where would you get the money?"

Was this his way of preparing me for a "no"? It must have been clear I had come to ask him for it. I couldn't help but lower my head and voice as I said, "I came here to ask you for the money, Jawad. I'll put the factory in your name."

I looked up at him. He didn't look at me. He examined the fingertips on his right hand as they touched those of his left. I examined them too: a ring with a little diamond and fingernails that revealed the skills of the manicurist who took care of them.

It felt as if hours passed before he finally said, "The land is in your name. If I pay the construction and equipment expenses, only the factory would be mine. What if your venture fails? You wouldn't lose anything, but I'd lose everything I lent you."

"But it won't fail. I've done my research."

Did my boldness come from a sense that Jawad was belittling me? Doubting my capabilities because I wasn't as successful as he—through opportunism and soft-soaping of religious leaders and people of influence? Nevertheless, he was a success in people's eyes and in Huda's. And I needed him.

"Anything can happen, Sharif."

My mind started racing. How do I convince him? It didn't occur to me that for the past few days I had been hoping he would say no. His doubting my capabilities and his contempt were getting to me.

"I'll also put the land in your name," I said in response to his contemptuous challenge, but without really thinking. The smile that lit his face stabbed me. Was it a smile of satisfaction? Or was it of victory, in revenge for my past victories? What exactly had I won anyway? I felt bitterness, resentment, and despair.

"Great," he said. "Let's meet tomorrow at the notary public. You bring me the deed to the land, and I'll bring you the money you need, a certified check of course."

Through the haze from his huge cigar and from my agony, too, I heard his voice and mine agree on the amount, time, and place . . . then I left.

The land was my mother's. My father had put it in my name, but he had asked me not to touch it as long as my mother was still alive. But I was doing it now. Out of greed? In defense of my dignity? What if Jawad's fears came true? What would I tell Mom? I decided not to mention anything to her or Huda. They had no way of knowing it wouldn't be mine anymore. The most important thing was getting started with my venture. I would pay off my debts and buy back my land.

The streets were empty even though it was only four. The stores were closed. Why should they be open? People weren't buying anything except for food . . . and maybe some clothes. Once again I was full of fears. I crossed the street. Trash was piled on the sidewalk and part of the street. I avoided it and hurried to my car. More trash lay before me and . . . what was that? I stopped. A rat the size of a kitten was scurrying in the trash. At least it wasn't going through an economic crisis. I felt my lips form a smirk. I stood contemplating the rat, and he stood contemplating me. He raised his little head and stared at me with guttery eyes: boldly, maybe even provocatively, I thought. Even the rats were challenging me, I thought, and rightly so. The city had become theirs. They didn't flee as some of its other residents had done. They didn't demolish it like other residents—and nonresidents. The rat stood frozen, his eyes fixed on me, the insolent intruder who dared share his kingdom. I went on my way. Rats were kings in our city, as were the militias. What if the battles broke out again before the factory was built and before it started producing? No, the factory would be far from the battles. If it didn't produce today, it would tomorrow or the day after.

⸺ ⸺ The man remained silent as he contemplated the place, walking around it and examining it from all its angles—with Sharif al-Mukhtar behind him, silent too.

⸺ ⸺ All those months I didn't say anything about the land, but I did tell Huda I had quit my job.

"Finally!" she said. "Tell me about the new job."

I sensed enthusiasm in her voice, something I had been missing for a long time. But her enthusiasm was gone as soon as I told her about my venture, when I confessed to her about the debt I had had to resort to.

"Jawad is a generous person," she said, "and he's your friend. But what if you can't pay him back?"

I didn't dare explain my friend's "generosity."

"Don't worry," I reassured her. "The factory will be productive. And production will yield profit."

The fighting broke out again, and in the middle of the shelling I was having to go check on the construction work.

"Please don't go, Sharif, please."

When she kept pleading, I'd yell, "You kept nagging me about my job, and now you're worried about me? I can't win with you." Eventually she'd shut up.

One time, after the usual arguing, I headed there. I was frightened. I drove, my ears trying to determine how far away the shelling was. My heart beat faster every time I felt—or did I imagine it?—that the shelling was getting closer. Fortunately, I was driving between tall buildings, sheltered. But soon I passed the last of them, and again I was unprotected on the open road. Finally I arrived. Everything was fine. The construction was about to be completed. In a week, the machines would arrive. If the battles subsided, we'd be able to install them right away, and the production would start. I had four clients already, and one client would lead to another.

The sound of bombs getting closer and increased shelling interrupted my dreams. Should I take shelter there, behind the concrete or go back? What if the bombing increased? I ran to the car, the sweat of fear running down my face and making my clothes stick to my back. It was all her fault. If it weren't for her nagging, her insinuations, I wouldn't be facing death now. I wished for death! How could she complain that the salary from my job was too small? What would she do if I came back to her blind or paralyzed? What would I do? Death is deliverance, an end. What about blindness? Deformity? A lost arm or leg?

My fears made me speed, as if speed could save me from a bomb—as if a bomb couldn't chase or reach a fast car. I laughed at myself, but I kept going fast through streets empty except for a few cars like mine. Finally I reached home. With a trembling hand, I turned off the engine. I remained seated, trying to regain some composure. Still, my legs were trembling as I climbed the stairs. My hand failed me as I tried the key in the keyhole, so I knocked at the door violently. I didn't stop knocking until she opened it.

"Thank God you're safe. I was worried sick about you."

"If only you'd been worried sick sooner!" I dropped into a chair in the living room, silent and consumed by thought. She disappeared. A few minutes later she came back with a glass of water.

"Rosewater will help you calm down," she said and pushed the glass in front of me. I didn't look at her, and I didn't say anything. I didn't take the glass.

"Have some water, Sharif. It'll relax you."

"Relax?" I yelled. "How can I relax when all I see are your looks of contempt? All I hear are your complaints. You keep holding me up to other people. Do you think that relaxes me?"

When she didn't answer, I got more agitated.

"If I get hit by shrapnel and it maims me, it will be your fault," I said. "And if it kills me, you'll be rid of me. Maybe that's what you want so that—"

"Sharif, please!" she yelled. "Are you crazy?"

"No, my dear. If I die, you can marry someone who can send you to Paris, who can buy you—"

"Shut up, Sharif. You know very well traveling is the last thing on my mind. All I care about is your safety."

"My safety?" I said. "My safety is your obstacle. I'm sure our dear friend Jawad won't hesitate this time around. He's learned his lesson."

"Sharif!" she yelled and left the room with the glass still in her hand.

She was the reason I was in debt; she was the source of my humiliation. I had stripped my mother of her land. Every day I was risking my life, and she claimed all she cared about was my safety. Did she take me for a fool?

⸺ ⸺ The man silently contemplated the building before him, then walked around it slowly, examining it.

"Do you want to go in?" Sharif asked him.

Without waiting for an answer, he stepped over the rubble.

— 4 —

HUDA AND DINA ARRIVED HOME. As usual, the power was out, and as usual Dina complained. "Couldn't you find an apartment on a lower floor?"

Huda said nothing. She climbed the stairs slowly, thinking about Ahmad. Was it Martyrs' Square that made her think of him? Was it Dina's griping about something that wasn't worth it? She went into the kitchen to make rice. She sifted the rice, washed it, and let it soak. She took out the green bean stew and some cucumbers, lettuce, and tomatoes from the fridge to make a salad.

◆ ◆ Had *my* griping been worth it? Did I deserve what happened? He hadn't wanted to understand why I was complaining. It wasn't about the money. It had pained me that he was depressed at his job. It had pained me to see him passive, resigned, desperate—that Sharif the motivated, optimistic, ambitious, and energetic had disappeared and that others less smart and capable had "succeeded," while he was discarded as a result of his honesty and loyalty.

"Success isn't about getting rich at all costs," he would say. True. But what about his passivity and then despair and surrender . . . weren't they a result of his feelings of failure? When I told him that, he yelled at me, "It's enough that you're ambitious, energetic, optimistic!" I knew he was frustrated and angry and felt like a failure, so I kept quiet. But I could feel his reproachful looks every time I sat down to my books, his suppressed blame every time I was getting ready to write. I'd feel guilty, close my books, and put my papers away. I'd suggest going down to the neighbors' or—if the battles had subsided—to a movie, but he'd always say no. I didn't know what to suggest or what to do anymore. His despair was the reason he said no to everything. Even though I realized this, I didn't know how to deal with it. I was helpless. I couldn't focus on my readings and research. All I could do was prepare lessons for my students, correct their homework, and read stories to Dina. I got worried when he told me about his business venture and the money he had borrowed. How long would it take to pay it off? What if he couldn't pay it off? He was great friends with Jawad, but how long could Jawad wait? Even though I was apprehensive, I was relieved to see him leave the house again, busy himself studying maps, do some auditing, and go to meet with an engineer or a contractor. I was relieved because I no longer saw him sleeping in his chair or reprimanding me with his eyes every time I opened a book. So I went back to my books and research. I had to finish my dissertation and defend it. Many professors had left Lebanon, so I had a chance to find a job at one of the universities and increase my income, but the battles had broken out again. My fears about his paying off his debts vanished behind my fears for his life as he risked it to go check on the factory.

"You can't protect the factory from missiles," I'd say. "You might, at least, try to protect your life." He wouldn't answer me. His angry looks blamed me for his risking his life, for his borrowing money. In the midst of our fights and fears, the construction was completed. The machines arrived and were installed. Then our fights and fears subsided because the battles did. Jawad came over for a visit.

"Congratulations, Sharif," he said. "When will production start?" Sharif didn't welcome him with his usual enthusiasm. He was burned out, no doubt. Or was he feeling embarrassed because of his debts? I tried to make up for Sharif's coldness, to express our gratitude for Jawad's helping Sharif in a time of need. I put my hand on Jawad's arm and said, "As soon as the machines are tested and Sharif makes sure the products are good . . . that they're not flawed . . . we'll have you over for dinner to celebrate." I looked at Sharif. Instead of the smile I was expecting, I heard him mumble something I couldn't catch. His face was red, and he lowered his eyes. Then he quickly left the room. I took my hand off Jawad's shoulder and looked at him, confused. "What's wrong with him?"

Jawad was silent for a few minutes before he laid his heavy hand on my shoulder and said, "Don't worry, dear. He'll stop being nervous when production starts."

Did I break down because I, too, was nervous and scared? Did I break down because I felt the wall between me and Sharif growing higher, thicker, leaving me with no one to lean on? My knees faltered, so I sat on the couch behind me, gasping and shaking with sobs. Tears that I failed to control burned my cheeks, so I hid my face in my arms.

"Huda, darling. Please."

It wasn't Sharif. Jawad had bent over me. I felt his big arms around my shoulders, his warmth trying to soothe me. A chill ran through my body, and I came back to my senses. I gently unlocked his arms and looked up to tell him. . . . My gaze fell on Sharif, silently watching us. As soon as our eyes met, he yelled at Jawad, "Get out! Get out of my house, you jerk! What are you doing, taking over my wife? Isn't it enough you've already taken over my land?" He started to attack Jawad, who extended his arms defensively.

"I don't want to take over anything," he said calmly. "If you've lost whatever you've lost, it's your fault." Then he walked away. Sharif kept watching him until he was gone. I stood there stupefied. He shifted his angry look to me. I couldn't understand what was going on. I hadn't done anything wrong.

"What land?" I asked. "What have you lost?"

Instead of answering me, he slapped me. Once. Again. Two slaps.

"At least I haven't lost my honor."

The slaps rang in my ears. I went crazy. "Are you saying I have?" It was my turn to yell. I rubbed my cheeks to ease the sting.

"I don't know."

"You liar," I yelled. "You know me."

"I used to know," he said. "I don't anymore."

I couldn't believe it was Sharif I was speaking to. What had happened to him? He had accused me of selfishness, of negligence, of a thousand other things, but he had never doubted my honor. Now he'd actually beaten me. So, it wasn't only the ignorant, the drunks, or the addicts who beat their wives. Even the educated and the "refined" did as well. Was he too worried to think straight? Was that why he doubted my honor at the mere sight of Jawad consoling me? His friend Jawad? To beat me! What could I have done to deserve that? It suddenly occurred to me that he was pointing fingers at me in order to divert suspicion from himself—"Eating me for lunch before I could eat him for dinner?" as the proverb says. Was he really meeting with an engineer or a contractor every time he left the house in the afternoon? He had blamed me for spending time with my books instead of with him. Could that have pushed him into looking for someone who'd take care of him? Had he found someone who gave him more time and attention? What about love? Had our love disappeared under our worries—our piles of worries? I didn't comment on his accusation or the beating. I thanked God that Dina wasn't home, that she hadn't seen her father hit and humiliate her mother. I decided to watch him closely, but that was futile.

When the fighting broke out again, we went back to the bomb shelter. On the second day, we heard a loud thumping at the door. We thought it was shelling at first, then we heard Salah yell, "People, there's someone at the door," and ran to open it. Through the light of his flashlight, we saw Hikmat Haddad, our neighbor from a nearby building. He looked pale, and his hands were shaking. Salah pulled him inside and closed the door of the shelter. He asked, "Everything all right, Hikmat?"

Our eyes were fixed on the man shaking before us. In a broken voice, he told us that his wife had been wounded by the shelling of the night before, that he had carried her to the hospital despite the missiles and the bombs, and that they'd called him from the hospital to tell him she had died.

"I have to go get her now because the morgue is crowded, and power's out even at the hospital."

"Now? Tonight?" Tawfiq and Sharif asked at the same time.

"That's why I came here to ask for help."

Salah, Sharif, and Tawfiq went with Hikmat. When they came back, they told us that before going to the hospital, they had bought a coffin. The coffin store was open twenty-four hours a day now that its business was booming. In the dark of the morgue, Hikmat identified his wife's body. They laid her in the coffin and transported her to the cemetery. They wouldn't let Hikmat go back to his house because it was destroyed, so he came back with them to our shelter. Hikmat's tragedy didn't make me forget what Sharif had done, but for the time being it took precedence in my mind. We stayed in the shelter for a few days. Sharif didn't talk to me, and I ignored him. If it was shame and regret that his silence hid, then he had to apologize. He didn't. He didn't say anything at all. Three days later the shelling stopped. We weren't sure whether we should leave or wait and see if the calm would last. Then out of nowhere there was a loud knock at the door. When Tawfiq opened it, our gaze fell on a man who just stood there. We looked at him and then at one another. No one recognized him.

"Is Mr. Hikmat Haddad here?" he asked, glancing around the room.

"Here," said our neighbor without moving from his seat among us.

"Can we step out for a minute?"

Hikmat hesitated, and we all recalled stories of others who had been taken for questioning by strangers and never came back. Wasn't his wife's tragedy enough? Tawfiq grabbed Hikmat's arm and said, "I'll go with you." The two men left, and we remained silent. Even the children withdrew into a corner of the shelter, speaking in low voices. Ten minutes passed before Tawfiq came back alone.

"What's the matter?" Our words came out as if from one mouth.

Tawfiq smiled, "I don't know whether we should laugh or cry."

"Over what?" his wife asked.

"There's a woman's body in the man's car," he explained. "When Hikmat saw it his face turned pale. His whole body started shaking and the words 'my wife' came through his quivering lips."

"The man stole his wife's corpse from the grave?" a bewildered Wafa' yelled.

"No, not at all," he said. "Apparently the body we buried was that of the man's wife. Hikmat thought it was his wife because of the darkness. Today when the man went to the hospital to collect his wife's body, they gave him Hikmat's wife. When he told them it wasn't his wife, they remembered that only one body had been retrieved two days ago, so they gave him Hikmat's name and address. He came so they could exchange their wives—their wives' bodies." Did we laugh? Cry? Neither. We packed our things in silence, and everybody went home.

"Don't go to school, Dina," Sharif said. "Let's wait one more day to make sure it's safe. I'm going to check on the factory." Then he left without talking to me, without even looking at me. As usual, I left Dina at the neighbors' and went to school to consult with my director, then to the university to return the books I had borrowed and get new ones. "The last batch of books," I thought, relieved that all I had to do was write my dissertation. At eleven o'clock, I went back home. I brought Dina from the neighbors' and went into the kitchen to make lunch. One o'clock, two o'clock. Sharif wasn't back yet. I had lunch with Dina, but was preoccupied. What had delayed him? Then it occurred to me: Had he gone to *her*? Did he miss her? Miss who? Who is she? I was getting nervous. "He can go to hell," I said to myself, trying to overcome my anxiety, but I couldn't help feeling jealous. Was I feeling jealous because I still loved him? Because he was my husband? Because I was his wife—a wife who, according to him, neglected her duties and paid attention to herself and her future instead of to him?

"Where's Dad? Why isn't he back yet?" Dina's questions pulled me away from my worries. I went to the bedroom to straighten up the drawers.

"Come pick up your toys," I yelled to Dina. Finally I heard his key in the door. I looked at my watch: four o'clock. Where had he been? I continued doing my work, but my blood was boiling, and all sorts of ideas were going through my head. I heard his footsteps getting close to the room, stopping at the door. I didn't lift my head to look at him, and I didn't say anything. I kept arranging the socks in the drawer. When I heard him close the bedroom door behind him, I looked up. His face was as white as a shroud. His eyes were red, emitting sparks. His arms—no, his whole body was shaking. It wasn't until then that I noticed his undone tie and ripped shirt.

"Sharif, what happened to you?" I cried and ran to him. He must have had an accident. Somebody must have attacked him.

"What happened to me? What happened to me?" His whole body was shivering. I was frightened both by his voice and by the way he looked. I worried he was about to have a fit or a heart attack. I couldn't move or talk. He fell in front of me and passed out.

"Dina, go get some water!" I yelled, bending over him. I unbuttoned his shirt, slapped his face, rubbed his temples.

"Call Uncle Tawfiq," I told Dina when she came with the water. I sprinkled it on his face as I heard Dina calling for help.

"Uncle Tawfiq, Uncle Tawfiq!"

Sharif opened his eyes before our neighbor arrived. I silently dried his face and neck, letting him calm down before I asked him again what happened. He remained quiet, dazed, and pale.

"What's the matter?" Tawfiq asked. "What happened?"

"I don't know, Tawfiq," I replied. "That's what he looked like when he arrived. Help me carry him to bed."

"I'll call a doctor right now."

Without saying a word, Sharif let us lift him off the floor and support him so he could stand up, walk slowly to his bed, and lie down. I covered him with a blanket and sat down to watch him while Tawfiq called the doctor. I didn't dare ask him again, and he didn't say anything. His eyes remained shut, and he was still as white as a ghost. I didn't find out what happened until the doctor arrived and started asking him questions. I felt the room turn around me and an iron hand clasp my brain, paralyzing my thoughts.

Sharif had parked his car in front a huge pile of rock and rubble in place of his factory, with the brand-new machines buried under it.

"I saw the debts, doctor, the debts that I won't be able to pay off and Mom's land that I had put in the name of my lender," he said. "I was choking. I undid my tie, but I couldn't undo the buttons of my shirt, so I ripped it so I could breathe. I wished I were dead that second, but I couldn't help ripping my shirt. I couldn't tell anymore if I wanted to die or try to live. . . . What is there to live for? Or who?"

"For your wife," the doctor replied calmly as he started examining him. "For your daughter."

So I, the wife, had become his scapegoat.

"It's all because of you," he said. "Because of your complaining, your nagging."

I said nothing.

"I'm lucky I've still got some brains, unlike you. I didn't quit my job. I just asked for some time off."

Again, I said nothing.

"I'm not ambitious like you," he said. "What kind of ambition is yours anyway? Ambition without risk, with guaranteed results."

I didn't say anything, but I couldn't get myself to concentrate on the dissertation I was writing.

"Of course, the land isn't yours," he said. "It's Mom's. You didn't lose anything."

Sometimes he was sarcastic. "When you become a great professor, are you going to give me, out of the kindness of your heart, something so I can retrieve my land from your dear friend?"

"He's more your friend than mine."

"My friend?" he said. "Someone who took advantage of my need in order to steal my land? No, my dear. He's not my friend."

"Why did you go to him then?" I asked without thinking. "Why did you ask him for help?"

"Because of you," he replied. "Because of your complaining, your nagging." The story would repeat itself, day after day, month after month. In the end, I couldn't take it anymore.

"What do you want me to do, Sharif?" I asked.

"You are doing things. Reading. Studying. Becoming a great professor who won't be satisfied to be the wife of a working man."

"Sharif, please—"

"Someone whom only a rich guy like Jawad would suit."

I stared at him in disbelief. "You know very well I rejected him from the beginning. For you."

"But he was poor then, and I was the smart, successful one. Not now, my dear. I saw you in that touching scene. Don't try to fool me after—"

I covered my ears and ran out of the room. I could understand his being stressed out because of the debts and the land; I could understand his taking it out on me because I was the one in his face, but how could he accuse me of such a thing? It occurred to me once again that he might be accusing me in order to divert suspicion from himself. I was a nervous wreck—thanks to his daily criticism, sarcasm, attacks, and insinuations. I didn't care anymore. So what if he was cheating on me? I had enough worries. I was also worried about Dina. I'd see her standing at the door, watching us fight. I'd read in her face the questions of a child who couldn't understand, who was aching and confused. I read all that in her face and kept quiet. Once she asked me, "Mom, are you going to leave me?"

"Never, honey," I said. "Why would I leave you?"

"Because Dad is mad at you."

I tried to explain to her calmly that he was tired and worried, and that she shouldn't be scared because no matter what happened, I wouldn't leave her.

"So is Dad going to leave us?"

Was I in a position to speak for him? I pulled her close to me so I didn't have to see the fear in her eyes and she the tears in mine. "Your dad loves you, Dina," I said. "As much as I do." I didn't answer for him, but I didn't lie either.

As usual, he left home at six-thirty to drop Dina off at school before going to his office. I finished doing the breakfast dishes and grabbed the books I had to return to the library before going to school. I tried to open the door, but it was locked. I thought that maybe Sharif had forgotten that I was in the house and had locked it by mistake. I opened my purse: my keys weren't there. I went back to our bedroom and looked in my other purses, in my drawers, under the furniture, in the kitchen, and in the other rooms. My keys had disappeared. Had I forgotten them at the grocery store the day before? I called the store, and they said they hadn't found any keys. I hadn't been out of the house since getting back from the store, so the keys had to be here. I worried about school. I didn't know what to do. I called in sick and decided to clean up the house, hoping they'd turn up somewhere. I moved the beds, chairs, and tables and swept and mopped under them. Then I dusted the chairs, tables, and books. I moved the dressers, the fridge, and the oven and shook out the pillows and the carpet, thinking sarcastically that Sharif couldn't accuse me anymore of neglecting the house. Still, there was no trace of my keys. I would have to make copies of Sharif's keys. What if they had fallen into a burglar's hands? I told myself we had to change the locks. At one-thirty, Sharif was back with Dina.

"You locked me in by mistake, Sharif," I said, "and I've lost my keys. I couldn't go to school." He didn't say anything. I made lunch, and we sat down to eat. As usual, Dina started telling us stories about school: George had showed up in class after two weeks of absence because he had been sick, but Hania hadn't. The teacher told them Hania had been wounded by shrapnel in her head and that she was in the hospital.

"You think she's going to die, Mom?"

"No. Let's hope not," I tried to reassure her.

"The teacher said we can't visit Hania because she's in intensive care," and then, "What's intensive care, Dad?" When Sharif didn't answer her, I explained what it meant. After we were done eating, I started doing the dishes.

"Can you make me a copy of your keys?" I asked him. "Or should we change the locks?"

He grabbed the paper and went to his chair and unfolded it. I left the dishes and went to the living room. "The stores close early, Sharif," I told him. "Just give me your keys. I'll go make copies if you're too tired." He didn't answer and kept reading his paper.

"Sharif, can't you hear me?" This time I raised my voice.

"I can hear you," he said calmly without moving the paper from in front of his face. He didn't budge. I stood before him and said, "Give me your keys." When he didn't answer, I grabbed the paper from his hands and yelled, "Can't you hear me?"

"I told you I can hear you," he said, pushing me away with his foot. "I can hear you, but I don't want to give you my keys. This house is mine, and the house keys are mine." I was shocked. I suddenly realized that he had taken my keys and locked me in the house.

"Are you locking me up?" I yelled, feeling the blood rise to my head.

"It bothers you that you can't go out to meet your lover, doesn't it?"

"Shut up. You know very well I don't have a lover." I stood in front of him, shaking.

"I saw you with my own eyes," he said and went back to his paper.

"You're crazy, Sharif," I said. "The debts, the destruction of the factory, the loss of your land have driven you crazy. I don't know, but—"

"And you're going crazy because you can't go see him," he interrupted. He was fixed on that thought, and nothing could change his mind. Were his accusations quenching his thirst for revenge? Was he trying to put his blame on me because he felt guilty for his own actions toward his mother? Was he turning me into his accomplice? I could sense the futility of talking things over with him, of trying to convince him. The solution? Do I stay a prisoner? Stop going to work? I went back to my dishes. He had to come back to his senses. He couldn't keep me locked up like that. I thought of calling Jawad so he could convince Sharif of my innocence—our innocence—but I was worried my phone call would cause more suspicion and accusations. I decided to wait.

The next day he locked the door again. The phone rang. Should I pick up? What if it were somebody from school checking on me? What if it were a neighbor calling to borrow something? Do I expose my humiliation? What if it were Mom or my friend Sumaya? I didn't pick up. When he got back at one-thirty, he carried meat, vegetables, and fruit. I figured he was planning on keeping me locked up for a while. I didn't say anything. After lunch, I washed the vegetables and fruit, straightened up the kitchen, and waited for him to take his nap. I thought of grabbing his keys, unlocking the door, and running away. Then I thought of Dina. Should I grab the keys, make a copy, and come back? I knew he'd get up while I was gone. What would he do then? He could do whatever he wanted. I couldn't leave Dina. Suddenly it hit me that I could take Dina with me. We could run away together. We could go over to my parents'. I tiptoed to our room; I slid my hands into one of the pockets of the jacket he had hung on the back of a chair. I didn't find anything. I tried the other pocket, but there was nothing in it either. I gently lifted his jacket and felt the pockets of his pants. There was no trace of the keys. I cast him a spiteful look and left the room without making any noise. Should I tell someone? Who? How could I expose myself? For how long could I put up with this imprisonment? I didn't dare pick up the phone when he was gone. I didn't care anymore that they were probably talking about me at school—about the sick teacher who was never home.

    Two days later deliverance came from the place I least expected.

5

THEY WERE AT THE TABLE HAVING LUNCH. Huda was afraid her daughter might have been put off, that she would hesitate before agreeing to spend another weekend with her, that she would rather spend her weekends with friends her own age, listening to modern music or window-shopping at the jewelry and fancy clothing stores. It pained her that she couldn't convince her daughter it was all a waste of time—superficial fun.

"My friends and I are into that," Dina had said. "We're not from the Stone Age."

Huda knew shame had kept her daughter from adding the "like you" part. For the thousandth time, she wondered if her daughter's attitude would have been different if she'd raised her.

"Did you get bored sightseeing today?"

"Not at all, Mom," Dina said. "I wasn't crazy about going at first, but when we got there and looked around, when you explained things to me, I knew you were right. Now I'm starting to learn something about my city's past."

"Would you like to go sometime and visit some of the places we didn't get a chance to see today?" Huda asked, jumping at the precious opportunity. Her heart beat faster in anticipation. Maybe it was her chance to reach out to her daughter, to get her involved in her specialization, in the things she cared about. Maybe Dina would realize that she wasn't that different from her mother, that there were more similarities between the two of them than she thought. Naturally, she'd have liked for her daughter to be more serious, more inquisitive. If only Dina lived with her, she'd nurture that. . . . Did Sharif neglect that side in raising her so she wouldn't turn out like her mother—ambitious and "difficult"? Or was it her grandmother's fault, spoiling her more than necessary—letting her live as she pleased without ever saying no to any of her wishes? No, Huda couldn't blame the grandmother, who belonged to a different generation that had a different mentality. Maybe she thought that spoiling the girl would compensate for the loss of her mother.

Should Huda blame herself, then?

"I wouldn't mind," Dina replied. "We can do it next Saturday or Sunday."

Huda felt optimistic.

⸺ ⸺ I had felt the same optimism when the phone had rung that day.

"Youssif wants to consult you on a legal matter, Sharif," I said. "Should I tell him to stop by?"

He grabbed the phone and talked to his friend. "Sure, shall we say half an hour?"

Then he went back to the living room. I looked at my watch. It was four. The stores were closed. I went to the dining room, picked up my research papers and note cards and put them in a big envelope that I carried to the bedroom. Sharif was reading the paper. I wondered if he noticed what I had done, but he didn't ask any questions. When Youssif knocked at the door, Sharif opened it. I watched him from the corner of my eye, wondering if he would dare lock the door and take the key in front of a stranger. He didn't disappoint me. Sharif welcomed Youssif and shut the door, leaving the key in the lock. The two men went into the living room.

"Make us some coffee," Sharif ordered. I went to the kitchen, put the kettle on the stove, and made up my mind while I was waiting for the water to boil.

I served them the coffee and then went into the bedroom. Without creating any commotion, I grabbed a little bag and put my envelope and some clothes in it. I didn't care that Dina might ask where we were going or that she'd wonder about her father. She had no idea her father had locked me in the house, that he had accused me of something I hadn't done. I knew I'd figure out the answer—some answer—when she asked. I'd promised not leave her, so I wasn't going to do that. I closed the bag and picked it up, tiptoeing to Dina's room.

"Pack your books," I said, closing the door behind me.

She looked at me surprised. "I haven't finished my homework yet."

"You'll finish it at Grandma's," I said.

"We're going to Grandma's?" She jumped up, excited.

"Shh!" I said. "Dad's busy with his guest." I helped her pack her things. I put some of her clothes in my bag, strapped her backpack over her shoulders, and held her hand. I carried my bag with my other hand.

"How come you're taking a bag, Mom?"

"Sh! Keep quiet. Dad's working." I opened the door of her room and quickly pulled her to the hallway and then toward the door. Once again it was the guest who saved me. Sharif was busy explaining something and writing it down for Youssif. It was clear that Sharif did notice us leaving because he looked up from his paper and turned his head in our direction, but by then we'd gotten to the door. I opened it, and we left before Dina could get a chance to repeat her questions and before Sharif could say anything. Was it his pride that had stopped him from exposing us in front of a stranger? I ran down the stairs with Dina, my heart racing until we were inside the cab.

Dad opened the door for us. Dina ran to him. He picked her up and started kissing her, and she forgot about the bag question.

"What a nice surprise!"

"Who is it?" Mom's voice came from inside.

"It's us, Mom," I said. "Dina and I are here." It was after we went into the living room that my father noticed the bag I was carrying.

"What's that?" Mom asked, without hiding her surprise. Or was it disapproval?

"You don't want us to spend the night here?" I asked, putting on a pitiful, hurt face.

"Of course we do," Dad reassured me, as I had expected. "You're always welcome. Where's Sharif?"

"He has a guest," I said, keeping it brief. Then I looked at Dina.

"Come on," I told her, "finish your homework so you can eat dinner and go to bed."

Had my parents understood that I didn't want to talk about Sharif, about my unexpected visit? The important thing was that they not ask any more questions until Dina went to bed. Then I would tell them everything.

"Sharif has no right to lock you in the house," my father told me later, "but we don't approve of your running away with Dina. You and Dina belong at your home."

"Huda, men are the heads of their families," Mother said, "no matter what they do. A woman is worth nothing without her husband."

Her words got to me. I boiled with anger. How could a mother say that about her daughter? What an archaic mentality!

"Besides, it's your fault," she continued, her words piercing my heaving chest. "What good is more education going to do you? You've neglected him."

If my own mother was saying that, what would others say?

"Maybe I have neglected him, but it is only temporary," I said, trying to reason with them. "A higher degree means higher income, for me and for him."

"His income's been just enough, providing you with what you need, my daughter," my father explained. "You've insulted him by making him feel he's not good enough for you, that he can't meet your needs."

"There's nothing better than being content with what you have," my mother added. "A woman should be content with what her husband provides for her. She should respect him under any circumstance."

"Who's saying I don't respect him?" I said, agitated. "Striving for more doesn't mean I respect him less."

My mother's sharp, reprimanding looks tore through me.

"A man gets married so he can have a woman, a real housewife, to take care of him. It should be the last of his worries whether she's ambitious or not," my mother explained. "In fact, a man gets put off by a woman who wants to prove her superiority, to prove that she's better than him. No—"

"I don't want to prove my superiority, to prove that I'm better than others. I want to make a better life for us. That's all."

"And to show him that he can't do that," she said. "You're assaulting his manhood. You're humiliating him."

I shut up. It was impossible to convince someone whose logic was completely different from mine . . . from my generation's. . . . My generation? Wasn't Sharif from my generation? Or is a man's mentality the same across all generations?

"So you're not going to let us stay here?" I asked.

They didn't answer. They were kicking me out. Where would I go with my child? I was filled with self-pity.

"You're our only child, Huda," Dad finally said. "We can't kick you out. Tomorrow I'll call Sharif. I'll talk to him, and everything will go back to normal. You'll see."

How could I convince them that I couldn't take his constant reprimanding and daily accusations anymore? He held me responsible for his debts and for his land. Now he could add my escape to the list.

6

SHARIF OPENED HIS EYES, rubbed them, and looked at his watch.

"Are you up, dear?" His mother was standing at the door, holding a tray with his usual postnap cup of coffee.

"Is Dina back?"

"No, not yet."

She put his cup on the end table next to his bed and sat in the chair across from him, hoping he would tell her about his day, his work, his colleagues. Like every day, though, he sipped his coffee, silent and lost in thought. In the past, she had asked questions, to which he had only replied, "Fine," so she had stopped asking. Just as she had stopped asking him about what happened between him and Huda.

That day when she had opened the door, he had stood before her with his suitcase.

"I'm going to be living with you, Mom," was the only thing he said when he came in.

When she asked him what happened and if it was worth it to leave his wife and deprive his daughter of his affection, he said, "If I'm a burden on you, I'll just leave." Of course he wasn't a burden, but didn't she have the right to know?

"What about Dina?"

"I'll be seeing her. I'll have her over so you can see her too."

Then she decided to get it out of Dina—"Take their secrets from their children," as the proverb goes—but Dina just said, "Dad left the house."

"Why?"

"I don't know."

"Didn't you ask Mom?"

"We were at Grandma and Grandpa's. Then we went home, and Dad left."

Had they told Dina not to say anything? Or had they kept the truth from her? She was afraid of asking Sharif again and just hoped he'd read the questions in her eyes, in her sighs, every time she sat across from him at lunch and dinner. They were always silent and dejected. He didn't understand or say anything. Yes, he did. He had started staying out during the evening as well as at noon, until she forced herself to exchange her depressing silence for a fake smile.

Sharif put the empty cup on the tray and began to get dressed. He looked at his watch again. "Dina will be here in a few minutes, Mom."

She took the tray and left the room. He put his clothes on slowly.

⸺ ⸺ I left the room when I heard the doorbell. My blood was boiling, and my head was about to explode from the pain. I opened the door violently and froze when I saw Huda's father. I was expecting her—both of them.

"Can I come in, Sharif?" He entered before I answered and gently shut the door behind him.

"Where's Dina?" I asked. I was nervous and couldn't control the trembling in my arms.

He slowly walked to the couch and took off his coat. He put down his cane, took a seat, and looked at me calmly. "At our place. With Huda."

"Her home is here, not at your place. I want my daughter back."

"What about Huda, Sharif? You don't want *her* back?"

"Back? Why would I? What would I do with her?" I asked. "Watch her read and write instead of doing what she's supposed to do at home? Listen to her complain about the increase in the cost of living and my small salary? Because of her—"

"She's trying to increase your income in a decent way."

"Decent?" I yelled. "Is it decent for her to cheat on me? And with who? Jawad? So much for friendship."

I could see he wasn't pleased with what I said, but I kept going before he could object. "Don't tell me it's all in my head. I saw them myself. He was holding her in his arms, her head on his shoulders."

"Sharif, calm down. Your friend was trying to console her, to make her feel better. That's not cheating."

Of course he had to defend his daughter.

"When is it considered cheating? When she sleeps with him?"

"Sharif!"

"Please don't interrupt me. If she were really innocent, she wouldn't have run away."

"She ran away because you locked her up."

"I locked her up so she wouldn't keep cheating on me. Jawad stole my land because of her. You want me to keep quiet while he steals my wife too?"

He tried to convince me that Huda wasn't cheating on me and that she "loved" me. That she was doing everything she could for us—Dina and me—and wanted to come back home.

"I'm not stopping her," I said.

"Are you going to lock her up again?"

"That's my business. It's my house, and I can treat my wife however I want."

It wasn't until then that he started to lose his patience. "Then she's not coming back."

He stood up, put on his coat, and grabbed his cane. He left without looking at me, and I stayed in my place. They couldn't deprive me of my daughter. I waited for her for two days. On the third, I went to consult Samih, a friend of mine from law school. His specialty was personal affairs.

"Fortunately for you, she's the one who left the house. So it's her fault, not yours."

"Regardless of why she left the house?"

"The religious courts are in charge of these cases. They have the final say. They penalize a married woman who leaves her house. You haven't hurt your wife, you haven't threatened her life—"

"I locked her up. I threatened her freedom."

"She has to come back even if it's your fault. Besides, you have the right to stop her from cheating on you. The religious court takes that into consideration. Adultery is considered a valid reason for divorce, if it's a divorce you want."

Would a hug be considered adultery? I wondered to myself. How do I know they've only hugged? Reassured and confident, I left Samih's place.

Another week passed. Huda wasn't home yet, so I called our priest, who said, "Father Boutrus al-Hajj specializes in these cases, my son. You should go see him."

I did.

"Wives aren't allowed to leave their husbands. Saint Paul's message is clear," Father al-Hajj told me. "'Wives, submit to your husbands as to the Lord. For the husband is the head of the wife as Christ is the head of the church. . . . Now as the church submits to Christ, so also wives should submit to their husbands in everything.' I'll ask her to come, my son."

He did, but she didn't come alone. She was with someone I didn't know. I figured out from our first session it was her lawyer. How could she afford the fees? Jawad! He was the first person who came to my mind. I became more determined to prove that she had been cheating. Her lawyer used the Bible just as Father al-Hajj had done.

"But Saint Paul also said in that same passage, 'Husbands ought to love their wives as their own bodies. He who loves his wife loves himself.'"

"But the passage asks the wife to 'respect her husband' and 'submit to him,' not the other way round." So Huda had to come back to me and submit to my will. It was easy for me to prove that she wasn't taking care of me or our house. To which Huda—or rather her lawyer—responded that she wasn't neglecting me and that, in fact, she started working to help increase our income, that I changed after the fighting in the city increased, that I quit my job, and that I started mistreating her after I borrowed the money and the factory was bombed. The war and my despair had turned her into my scapegoat.

"She's nobody's scapegoat," I said. "If it weren't for my loyalty, I wouldn't have been able to put up with everything for years. But love can't survive when it's one-sided, when it's met with betrayal."

Huda and her lawyer couldn't convince the priest that she hadn't cheated on me. The facts that I saw her in a stranger's arms and that she had neglected me and my house were enough to tilt the verdict in my favor: we were to be separated, and I was to get custody of Dina. I also got to keep the house and everything in it. After all, it was Huda who had left the house and was refusing to come back.

"But Dina's still a child!" Huda yelled.

"She can stay with you until she's nine," the priest said. "Then her father will take her. You left the house. He didn't. If you cared about your daughter, you wouldn't have done that. Besides, she's his daughter."

"She's *my* daughter too," she yelled in the priest's face. It didn't matter. In the end, I was the winner again. After months of arguing and bargaining, evidence and counterevidence, I was the winner. Finally, Huda learned who the master was—learned who was in the right. "Separation" meant that she wasn't allowed to get married. I felt the pleasure of revenge against her and Jawad. What about Dina? Would I really have to wait for three years until she was mine? Would she be really mine if they poisoned her mind and turned her against me? No, they wouldn't be able to do that.

"I want to see Dina alone," I told Huda as we left the courtroom.

Instead of answering me, she looked at her lawyer.

"She's my daughter!" I yelled in her face. "Nobody can deprive me of seeing her whenever and however I want." I turned my back and left without waiting for an answer.

The next day my father-in-law brought me Dina. She jumped on me, and I held her in my arms. I kissed her head and smelled her neck, burying my face in her hair so she wouldn't see my tears. In glorifying motherhood, motherly love, people forget about fatherhood, fatherly love!

"Pick her up in an hour," I said as I closed the door behind him. Dina slipped away from my grasp and ran to her room. I waited for a while before I followed her. I stood at the door and silently watched. She had opened her bin of toys: she took out a doll, looked at it, pulled it close to her chest, and threw it to the floor at her feet. Then another doll. After taking everything out of the bin, she opened her closet and stood there for a few minutes looking at her clothes. Then she walked to her bed and rubbed the white bunny she slept with. She looked up at me.

"You won't let us come back home, Dad?"

They had started to poison her mind against me. How could I explain to her? Could a child understand? Could she understand that her home is still hers even if her father lived there by himself, that her father loved her more than anybody, even though he didn't live with her? What was her fault in all this?

"You won't?" she repeated.

"Of course I will, honey. You'll be back tomorrow. Grandpa's coming to pick you up in a little while."

That same night I packed my two suitcases. The next day I went to my mother's place and told Huda to come back with Dina to the house—to Dina's house.

⸺ ⸺ As soon as Sharif got dressed, he heard the doorbell. Who would it be but Dina? He left his room to open the door himself and kiss his daughter before going out. She'd been living with him for seven years, and he still couldn't go out until he saw her when she came home from school. It was a habit now—after being a necessity during the first year. It was necessary that Dina find him when she returned, that he stay with her until she fell asleep, that she see him when she woke up. That she felt his love and attention weren't less than those of her mother, who had left her.

⸺ ⸺ Huda opened the door for me. Dina was sitting down, with her two bags of clothes and toys next to her. She didn't run over to hug me as she usually did. Instead, she looked up at me with tearful eyes. Reproach, maybe. Or fear. Then she quickly lowered her eyes. I went to her and pulled her into my arms.

"Grandma's waiting for you, honey. She made you your favorite chocolate cake."

"I don't want to leave Mom! I don't want to go," she yelled, unlocked my arms, and looked at me, her eyes full of resentment—which Huda had planted, no doubt.

I looked at Huda. "Come on, talk to her. I'm her father."

In her eyes, I read a silent protest, as if she wanted to say, "And I'm her mother!"

Instead, she bent over and pulled Dina close to her. "Honey, remember what I told you about the law? That's the way it is."

Dina pushed her away, sobbing. "You don't love me. If you loved me you wouldn't leave me." Then she ran toward the door, opened it, and left. Without saying anything, I picked up her bags and hurried after her.

In the car, Dina didn't say a word as sobs shook her tiny body. Should I talk, or should I keep quiet like her? I didn't know what to do. In the end, I chose to keep quiet.

Mom opened the door for us. "Hi, sweetie," she said, bending over to hug Dina, who avoided her arms, ran to her room, and slammed the door behind her.

"Don't blame her, Mom," I said when she looked at me, disappointed. "She's just a child. She'll get used to us."

"I can't blame her, Sharif," she said. "Have you forgotten that our grandchildren are dearer to our hearts than our own children? I'm just worried I won't be able to convince her that we also love her."

"Don't worry, Mom. She'll be convinced soon."

I drove her to school in the mornings. At two, I'd wait for her, and we'd go home together. I stayed with her while she studied and didn't leave the house until she went to bed. Mom always made her favorite meals and dessert.

"Wow, Grandma! Everything you make is yummy!"

"Have some more!"

"Not like Mom's food. She makes me eat everything, even stuff I don't like."

We felt the ice starting to break. The fact that I never said no to any of her wishes must have helped, too. When she coveted a friend's doll, I'd buy her one. When she wanted to see a movie, I'd take her and her friends. When she mentioned that Randa wore a new dress, I'd ask Mom to take her to buy herself a new dress. At night, I would meet with a defendant and settle his case with an opposing party; I'd mediate between brothers quarrelling over inheritance; I'd write official requests for whoever needed them. That's how I made my living now. I no longer heard Dina's sobs before she fell asleep—when she thought nobody could hear her—or the unconscious wails she made during her dreams. They didn't go away suddenly, nor did they stop at the same time. Every Sunday evening, when I picked her up from Huda's, I saw the tears she tried to hold back. At night, I heard the wails that disturbed her dreams. I was also disturbed every time I saw her glued to Huda until the last minute. She wouldn't let go of her until I got upset and looked at my watch, saying, "Come on, Dina."

Then one Sunday she ran to me when I came to pick her up. She gave her mom a quick kiss on the cheek, and without hugs or loitering she beat me to the stairs.

"God, Dad! Mom's so boring!" she said as soon as we were in the car. "All she wants to do is read me stories or go for walks and pick flowers. She wants me to memorize the names of flowers. Like I don't already have enough things to study."

I was really happy. Finally, Dina felt she belonged with me. When she became a teenager, my happiness was mixed with malicious joy every time she complained of having to spend time at Huda's.

"Why does she have to be a teacher all the time?" she once said. "She has to teach me something new all the time. All she can think of for things to do is an exhibition or a play or a concert."

⸻ "Hi, sweetie." Sharif kissed her on the cheeks.

"Dad, I don't have that much homework, and my friends are going to the movies tonight. Can I go, too?"

"Of course, honey. I just want you to be happy."

"You're the best dad in the world!" she said, throwing her arms around his neck. "I'm going to stay with you forever!"

Sharif smiled and watched her run to the phone. He put his coat on and left without listening to what his daughter was saying.

7

HUDA WAS IN HER OFFICE preparing questions for the monthly exams when a soft knock interrupted her train of thought. When she opened the door, a pale, skinny young man dressed in faded shirt and jeans stood before her.

He hesitated. "Is this Dr. Halim Nasser's office?"

"It used to be. He moved the day before yesterday."

"Could you please tell me where?"

"It's on the second floor, room number . . . ugh! I don't think he is in today. Anyway, let's go ask the secretary."

When it turned out that Halim was really absent that day, Huda told the young man, "Come back tomorrow. He'll be in his office at ten."

He hesitated for a minute. "I can't come tomorrow. I don't know when I can come back."

"Who should I say asked for him?"

He froze for a moment before saying, "Please tell him Qasim Ali came by . . . if he still remembers me."

"Sure," Huda answered without thinking, and the young man left. A moment later she froze: Qasim Ali?! She ran after him, but he was gone. She asked some students and employees, but no one had seen him. She went back to her office, angry with herself. Hadn't Halim come to see me that day to talk to her about a student—perhaps Qasim Ali? Or had there been another reason?

⁓ ⁓ Dina had gone to bed, and I was in my room preparing my lessons for the next day when the phone rang.

"Huda? You're home then."

I recognized his voice right away, "Where else would I be, Halim? Of course I'm home."

"Okay. I'll be right over."

I was both bothered and not by the unexpected visit. I had to prepare a lesson, so now I was going to have to get up early in the morning, but I was pleased that my two friends were coming over—especially these old friends from college. Nobody else visited me since Sharif had left. I imagined what men told their wives about me: "We don't want you hanging out with the woman who left her husband." They didn't want me rubbing off on their wives, corrupting their subservience. As for the women, they feared for their husbands—the single, lonely woman was a danger. People no longer invited me for lunch or dinner at their homes.

I left my books and papers, straightened up the living room, prepared the kettle, coffee, and sugar, and set some cups on a tray. As I finished, the doorbell rang.

"Hi, Halim." I looked behind him. He was alone. "Where's Sumaya?"

"She couldn't make it, so I came alone."

He came in and shut the door behind him. I didn't move, and my heart started beating quickly. He had never come over alone. Did Sumaya know he was at my place? Weren't people finally convinced that I was innocent of what Sharif had accused me? I never saw Jawad after that day. I never had him over, or anyone else for that matter, after Sharif left us. Didn't they know me better than to think I was like one of those women? Or did they just assume every lonely woman is easy prey sooner or later?

"What's the matter, Huda?"

He'd taken his coat off and sat down on the couch where he usually did. He looked at me, his eyes full of innocent surprise. Had I misjudged him, or had he faked this surprise and innocence? I remained standing, as thoughts raced and clashed in my head. If I believed in his innocence, he might cross the line, and I would have to put an end to our friendship. What if I didn't believe in his innocence and asked him to leave? Wouldn't that end our friendship too? Whatever was to happen would happen.

"I'm sorry, Halim. I can't have you in my house alone," I said and reached for the doorknob.

"Come on, Huda. I'm like your brother! I came here to unburden my soul to you. I'm concerned about a student of mine. Qasim Ali has suddenly disappeared from school, and he's sent me—"

"Please, Halim. You can tell me about him tomorrow, at school."

"You don't trust me?"

"I totally trust you," I said firmly. "But the neighbors! What will they say? They don't know you. And even if they did, I have a daughter. I don't want them saying things about me that might hurt Dina."

I opened the door and prayed that nobody had seen his coming and going. I could see he was upset as he grabbed his coat and put it on.

"Dina's a child. What reputation are you worried about?"

"You know what they say, 'The apple doesn't fall far from the tree,'" I said. "People have merciless tongues, especially when it comes to a woman whose husband has left." I hurried outside so he wouldn't linger or do anything that might look as if we were intimate.

I couldn't concentrate when I got back to my lesson plans. Even one of my dearest and oldest friends was trying to take advantage of me, despite my friendship with his wife. Or was it because of that friendship? Did he think our friendship would make people less suspicious? Did he want to use me? I could understand others wanting to use me because I was a woman living by herself. But my friend?

"The lease is in Mr. Sharif's name, ma'am. He doesn't live here anymore."

"I'm his wife," I told the landlord, who had come knocking at my door six months after Sharif left me.

"He left you," he said, looking at me with contempt. I didn't ask him to come in, and he remained standing at the door. I knew he wanted to evict me so he could get a higher rent for his apartment.

"But he let me stay here with my daughter." The word "let" stabbed my dignity. The only reason I could stay in my home was that Sharif "let" me. Now it was for the landlord to "let" me too.

"He let you, but I didn't. This is my apartment."

He thought that I was weak because I was alone and that he could take advantage of me. I said firmly, "The apartment is yours, but my husband rented it, and he's still paying rent. If you have any objections, go ahead and contact him . . . good-bye." I slammed the door before he could say anything else.

When I saw Halim the following day, I greeted him as if nothing had happened.

"So, what's the story with that student who disappeared?" I asked, picking up our conversation from the day before.

He, too, pretended as if nothing had happened and said, "I don't know. He's one of my best students. He disappeared a week before the semester was over. When I left class, a young man I don't know came up to me and handed me a form. He said, 'Please, sir, could you sign this withdrawal form for Qasim Ali?' I studied his face, looked at the form, and said, 'Where's Qasim? He has to turn this in himself.' The young man got nervous. After looking right and left, he whispered, 'No way. He can't come. I'm even taking a risk by coming here. I have to go now. Please, sir.' His eyes were pitiful, so I took the form. It had Qasim's name and the courses he was taking. Next to each course was the signature of every consenting teacher, except for mine."

"But he's an excellent student?" I asked, surprised.

"Yes, he's an excellent student. That's what I told the young man, but he insisted it was better for Qasim to get an incomplete than a zero on his final exams for not taking them. I looked at my colleagues' signatures. Did they sign it because they knew something I didn't? Was it logical for Qasim to waste a whole semester's worth of fees, effort, and excellent grades?"

"What did you do?"

"I didn't sign it. I gave the young man my number and asked him to tell Qasim to call me."

"Did he call?" I asked. "Did you find out what his story was?"

"After he took my number, the young man kept standing there. He said he couldn't come back for my signature. Then I remembered my course doesn't require a final exam since the students have enough grades for work throughout the semester. So I told him I'd ask the administration to waive that requirement. That way Qasim would get the grade he deserved. And that was that."

"What about Qasim? Did you hear anything from him or about him? His story?"

"That's why I came to your house yesterday. I wanted to ask if you've ever had him as a student, if you knew anything about him."

I studied his face. There was no anxiety, reprimand, or agitation. At least, none that I could detect. I felt things were back to normal between us. "No, I don't know anything at all."

Two weeks later Halim stopped me in the courtyard at the university. "Huda, I heard from Qasim. I was grading papers when Sumaya told me someone was on the phone and wanted to talk to me."

"Was it Qasim?"

"I never knew we could have such an influence on our students. Not all of them, of course. As soon as Qasim heard my voice on the phone, he said, 'Sir, it's been two weeks, but it feels more like two years. I miss the university. I miss my classmates and my professors. I even miss the smell of the hallway, the . . . ,' then his voice choked."

"You didn't ask him why he's disappeared?"

"I was afraid of asking questions over the phone. I assumed he'd disappeared for political reasons, even though I never sensed he had any political affiliations or that he cared for politics more than anybody else. That's why I told him to meet me."

"Did he? Were you able to see him?"

Halim looked at me, surprised. "Huda, you don't even know him. Why do you care about him so much?"

Was I worried that Ahmad's tragedy with the Israelis would repeat itself, this time at the hands of non-Israelis? Was I worried Qasim's back would be like Khalil's? Khalil was absent from school for six months; when he'd returned, I asked him why he was absent. He lifted his shirt and exposed his back: dark red lines and scars wide as a finger crisscrossed from top to bottom, making his skin look like a strainer.

"Have you forgotten Ahmad? I'm worried Qasim's going to end up like him."

"We set a time and place for our meeting. I got in my car and headed for the place, but the traffic was unbearable. I was worried I was going to be late and that Qasim would lose hope and leave before I could see him. A long line of cars barely moving stretched ahead of me. I looked at my watch: fifteen minutes and I was still in the same place. Have they ever arrested an armed person or a drug or weapon smuggler in these long lines at checkpoints? I entertained myself by watching pedestrians, wishing I were one of them."

I remembered how nervous I was the day Dina fell, how I carried her—like a crazy woman—blood gushing from her forehead. I kept telling the driver to bypass the line of cars at the checkpoint. "We have an injured person," I said. "You're excused." Booby-trapped cars that no checkpoint detected had been exploding west and east of Beirut. It made me realize the goal of these checkpoints was to delay *us*, the citizens—to break *us*.

Halim interrupted my thoughts. "I was startled by a soft knock at my window. It was an old lady carrying a big bag on her shoulders. When I rolled down the passenger side window, she asked me to drive her to the end of the road where her son was waiting. I unlocked the door for her, and she got in. She stunk. I opened my window. The dust from the street and the exhaust from the line of cars were more bearable than that woman's smell. When we got to the checkpoint, the soldier asked, 'What's in the bag?' I then realized I hadn't asked myself that question. I just didn't suspect her of anything. 'My clothes,' she said and opened the bag for him. I sighed. 'What's in that?' He asked, pointing to the briefcase in the backseat. I told him, 'My books. Would you like me to open it for you?' But he said, 'Open the trunk, please.' In the middle of all this, I was thinking about Qasim, waiting for me—or giving up hope. The soldier had to check my trunk to make sure I wasn't smuggling drugs or weapons, but how could he be sure my car wasn't booby-trapped? I didn't dare ask and moved along when he gave me the okay. I couldn't wait to get rid of the odor beside me. . . . "

"What about Qasim?" I interrupted. "Was he waiting for you? Did you find him? I'm not one of your students, Halim. Why are you telling me all these details?" The images of Ahmad and Khalil hadn't left my mind.

"For suspense," he laughed. "Yes, he was waiting for me. He got in the car, then I continued driving. He's always been pale and skinny, but this time it was worse. 'How are you, Qasim?' I asked. He didn't say anything. Where should I take him? I kept going straight, and neither of us said a word. When the street widened, I pulled on the right and parked the car. 'So, what happened?' I asked, wondering why he would trust me. I was just one of many teachers he knew. All he had to say was, 'I had to run away.' I said, 'I never thought you were a member of any party or that you were politically involved in any opposition movement.' Right away he said, 'Sir, I have nothing to do with politics or political parties. All I care about is learning and getting a degree—'"

I interrupted Halim again: "So who was he running away from? Why?"

"That's the strange thing about his story. He told me he wasn't from Beirut and his scholarship didn't cover his living expenses, so he had a night job at a restaurant."

"A cook?"

Halim laughed. "That's exactly what I asked." Then he smiled bitterly, "I wish! No, he washed dishes and ate the customers' leftovers. And I could tell by the way he looked that there weren't many. He slept in the stockroom where he also worked as a night watchman. A month ago he was getting the tables ready for dinner when three men came in and asked about an Imad Ali."

"Imad or Qasim?"

"Imad. It's his little brother in the village. He confirmed to them that there was no Imad Ali there, but they threatened to break his bones if they found out he was lying. They said they'd be back. He was worried they'd notice the change in his color, the trembling in his hands. He knew they couldn't be looking for his ten-year-old brother and had to be looking for him, so he packed his things and ran away."

"What did they want from him, though?"

"That's exactly what I asked. He didn't know and was afraid of waiting for them to return, so he just disappeared. Of course, I asked him where he was staying in the meantime. He said at his cousin's friend's house. He's also looking for a job, any job. His friend is a cabdriver and has seven kids, so Qasim can't burden him any longer."

"Can't he get an education at another university?" I asked without thinking. I realized how stupid my question was even before Halim answered.

"He's lost his scholarship. Obviously, he can't afford it."

"What about the Lebanese University? Why doesn't he go to one of its branches in another area?"

"I asked the same thing, too. He said the curriculum is totally different, and the two years he spent at our university would go to waste."

"Isn't it better than wasting his whole future?"

"He's young, Huda. Like any other young man, he thinks two years of his life are so important—until life teaches him otherwise. The most upsetting thing about his story is that a smart, innocent student can't prove his innocence. He's not even given a chance to prove it. In other countries, a suspect is considered innocent until proven guilty. But in our country an innocent person is considered guilty and isn't even given the right to prove his innocence. Qasim isn't just innocent. He's a dignified and honest person. It's very rare to find people like him these days."

Poor guy, I thought to myself. Where have dignity and honesty got Sharif? Where have they got me? And what about the opposite case—Jawad?

"A relative of his who works at an embassy called and offered him an overseas scholarship through the embassy, but he turned it down even though he really needs the money and wants to get an education."

"Turned it down? Why?"

"'Because nothing's free' is what he said. He doesn't want some foreign government to take advantage of him in exchange for the scholarship. Anyway, the important thing is that he called me two weeks later, and we met again. He got a job."

"Great!" I said spontaneously.

"If only you knew what kind of job! He sells gardenia necklaces at intersections!"

He was like hundreds of students the war had tossed on the streets, who dropped out of school or couldn't find a job even though they had degrees. They were working as laborers or selling vegetables . . . or gardenias.

"I was surprised he could make a living selling gardenias. When I asked him, he smiled and said, 'I wasn't expecting that either, but I've been making thousands of liras every week. You can't imagine, sir, how many men, young and old, stop to buy a necklace for their date in spite of the war . . . when the situation is stable, that is.'"

"Do you ever buy Sumaya a necklace when she's with you?" I joked with Halim.

"No," he laughed.

"Sharif didn't, either. He never bought me a necklace when we were married or even when we were engaged. . . . Maybe education dries up the emotions."

I remembered that Sharif and Ahmad would have said that about me.

"No, not emotions. Maybe it makes us forget the small things."

"They might be small, Halim, but they're sweet . . . and sometimes necessary. It's the small things that make up life."

I grew quiet, and Halim did, too.

A few weeks later Sumaya called me in the evening. "I have some bad news, Huda. Your dean's mother passed away. Halim wanted me to tell you that the burial is going to be tomorrow afternoon."

I told Dina I was going to leave her at Mom's so I could attend the burial.

"A bomb killed her?" Dina asked calmly, without lifting her head from the doll she was dressing.

"No, honey. People don't just die from bombs. She was old and very sick."

"Like Grandpa?"

"Yes, like Grandpa."

"Are you going to die when you're older?"

"We're all going to die, Dina. But don't worry. I'm still young, and by the time I'm old, you'll be all grown up. You'll be as old as I am now."

"But I want to stay with you, Mom. Grandma Umm Sharif is old, and Dad's still living with her."

Should I lie to her? Should I tell her she'll be living with me only for another year?

I told her to pack her books so she could study at Grandma's.

The church was full of people: colleagues and students I knew, relatives of the deceased, and her friends and acquaintances whom I didn't know. As usual, I half-listened to the prayers for the dead and the Scriptures. Like others, I had attended out of courtesy rather than sadness for someone I didn't know. Then I drifted into my sad memories of the dearest person I have ever known. That day, too, I didn't listen to the prayers of the dead or the Scriptures. I listened to Mom's sobs beside me, trying to hold back my own sobs that made my body shiver as tears slid down my cheeks. Then when the priest started eulogizing Dad, I listened. The comments were superficial and general. Why don't they ask someone close to the deceased to eulogize him—someone who knows him well, whose words would be specific to him, telling people about some unknown, important stops in his life and his lovable traits?

Now the priest stood, eulogizing someone I didn't know, so I paid attention. He talked about her late husband, his patriotic struggles and his suspension from his job by the French as a result of his patriotic stances, and about her son, who followed in his father's footsteps—his distinguished academic achievement as a student, his resistance to the temptations of universities in the West, his return to serve his country, his scholarly achievements that earned him his current position, his . . . his. . . . I listened attentively: When will the deceased's turn arrive? Didn't the poor woman deserve any credit for being there for her struggling husband and for taking care of her family after he was fired from his job? Didn't she play a role in raising the children—her excellent son? I looked at my watch: twenty minutes had passed, and the priest was still listing the son's virtues after listing his father's. Then, as if the preacher had read my mind, he said, "On behalf of our bishop and the parish, I offer our condolences to the family of the deceased for their great loss. They have lost a virtuous woman. She was a good wife and a good mother." A supplement, that was it, and the service was over—a eulogy for the husband who had passed away two decades ago and praise of the son attending the service.

The next day we went to offer our condolences at the dean's. The room was crowded with mourners. Since Sumaya, Halim, and I didn't know most of them, we withdrew to a corner.

"Have you heard from Qasim?" I whispered in his ear.

"I'll tell you later," he whispered back.

When we left together, Sumaya suggested, "Huda, why don't you come with us?"

"Dina's at Mom's. I have to take her home."

Sumaya looked at her watch. "It's still early. It'll be a nice change of scenery. You can pick her up in an hour."

It was too tempting. People didn't invite me to their homes anymore, so I agreed.

I went into the kitchen with Sumaya to help her make coffee, and when we came out to sit with Halim, I asked him again, "How's Qasim?"

"When I met him again, he told me he found a better job, washing dishes at a fancy restaurant that offered him food and a place to stay. The owner of the restaurant promised to promote him to waiter since 'dishwashers at restaurants aren't usually college students,' Qasim told me jokingly, without any bitterness or resentment. I had brought him a book so he'd keep reading. His smile encouraged me to take it out of the bag and give it to him. I told him it was an English novel, so he wouldn't forget the language, and I asked him if he had any time for reading. He said the restaurant was closed on Mondays, and he took the book."

"Did you find out what restaurant, so we can go there for dinner?" Sumaya asked. "To show our support?"

Before her husband could answer, I said, "Wouldn't you think it would be a little embarrassing or humiliating for him? To be our waiter instead of our student?"

Sumaya answered right away, "All the students in America wait tables during the holidays to make some money."

"That's America, Sumaya. There's a different attitude here."

"I don't think it would bother him at all," Halim interjected. "I gave him a ride to the restaurant. It had an Oriental design and big, archlike tinted windows with thin, black, wavy bars. Qasim insisted I go in and have a cup of coffee with him. The first thing that came to my mind was that he wanted to show the owner of the restaurant and his fellow waiters that he was different. That his connections were university professors. Then I felt bad for thinking that. He just wanted to thank me for looking out for him, and that was the only way he could do it."

Then we talked about other things—I forget what—until it was time for me to pick up Dina and go home.

After that, I started asking about Qasim every time I ran into Halim. I cared about him, and he became important to me. Was it because of his tragedy? His honesty? His dignity? Halim met him twice again and lent him some more books. When the fighting broke out again, I thought about Qasim, too, not just about my friends and acquaintances. In the bomb shelter, we turned a transistor radio on and listened for places where bombs were falling, neighborhoods under attack, the names of casualties. What about those people away from their neighborhoods and villages, like Qasim? Would anyone know his name to mention it if he got hurt? I prayed that no shrapnel had amputated a leg or an arm of someone I knew, that it hadn't paralyzed him or torn out his eyes, that it hadn't gotten him in the head or heart . . . so he would be gone. What about the names I heard of people I didn't know? Weren't they humans, with families and loved ones, mothers, fathers, and children? It was my selfishness, that human selfishness. The attack was over, and, like sheep, we all went back to our houses. We checked for broken glass, split doors, holes in the walls. And, of course, we checked on our friends and acquaintances.

"Have you heard from Qasim?" was the first thing I asked Halim after he told me his family was okay.

"No, nothing from him."

"You want to go check on him?"

He looked at me, surprised. I said, "If you don't want to go alone, Sumaya and I can go with you. His neighborhood was under attack for a long time." We decided to go there the following day.

Halim parked his car, and we walked the rest of the way because the roads were blocked with collapsed walls. We stood in front of what used to be the restaurant: broken glass, rubble instead of walls, and an entrance blocked by a fallen door. We stepped over the piles of stones and shards of glass and went inside. Broken chairs and tables . . . hissing, meowing. When I looked around, I saw a cat jump from a table and scurry outside. There was no other trace of life in there.

"Maybe they're in the kitchen or basement," Sumaya said.

I yelled, "Sir!"

"Qasim!" Halim yelled. "Qasim!"

Nobody responded except for the echoes of our voices in the deserted place. Was Qasim dead? I didn't dare say it out loud.

"Do you think he ran away?" I asked. "You think they got him?"

"They're definitely busy now with something more important than Qasim. Maybe he escaped to someplace safe."

Did he say that to reassure me? Or was he just reassuring himself? We looked around the restaurant one more time, then went back to the car without saying a word. Halim never heard from Qasim after that, and I never asked about him again.

⬥ ⬥ Huda remained frozen in her chair. At least Qasim was alive and not maimed. How could she have let him get away? How could she not have asked him where he lived and how he could be reached? The important thing was that he wasn't hurt. Now she could tell Halim he was fine. Then the phone rang, interrupting her thoughts.

"Hello. This is Huda Sabuh."

"Huda, Dina's sick. I won't be bringing her to your place for the weekend."

"Sick? What's wrong with her, Sharif?"

"What? She's never gotten sick with you?"

Should she tell him she wasn't blaming or accusing him of not taking care of Dina? His defensiveness confirmed to her that it would be pointless.

"It's the flu," he said. "Nothing serious. The doctor came and prescribed some things for her."

"Give her lots of fluids, Sharif," Huda said. "You have to force her to drink them. I'll come by to check on her after my lecture."

"Don't worry. Mom's here with her."

Why the cold tone? Was it to make her feel guilty? His mother was with Dina while Dina's mother was busy with her job, with others?

They had deprived her of her daughter, and now they were blaming her for it.

"I'll stop by at three this afternoon."

She hung up.

The image of Qasim faded from her mind, as did the words on the papers in front of her. She looked at her watch. Her last lecture was in an hour, then she could see her daughter. She put the papers back in the drawer and went to the university coffee shop.

8

UMM SHARIF OPENED THE DOOR FOR HER. A cold welcome. No smile. Was it to make Huda feel neglectful of her daughter? Was it because her mother-in-law held her responsible for wrecking her son's house? Huda had never forgotten her husband's blame whenever he came home after visiting his mother: "You haven't made dinner yet?" or "The shirt I want to wear is not ironed!" or, sliding his hand over the tables, "How long has it been since you've dusted?"

"Auntie," Huda asked, "how's Dina?"

"You can see for yourself," Umm Sharif said and walked ahead of Huda to her daughter's room. Dina was on the bed, her head and the upper half of her body propped up against two pillows. Her cheeks were flushed. Because of the sweat, her hair was stuck to her forehead and temples. Her eyes were shut. Huda thought she was asleep, until spotting the tiny earphones of the Walkman her daughter never parted with. Huda came closer and put her hand on the relaxed hand on the bed sheet.

"Dina?"

Dina didn't hear her mother, but she felt her hand and opened her eyes. She pulled out the earphones. "Will you be here for a while, Mom?"

Before Huda could say anything, Umm Sharif said, "Just for a second." She remained standing by the door.

"Where's your dad?" Huda asked.

Once again Umm Sharif answered, "He went to the drugstore. We're out of aspirin."

Huda felt her daughter's forehead. "What's her temperature, Auntie?"

"Thirty-nine Centigrade, Mom," Dina answered. "Dad took my temperature before he left."

Umm Sharif left the room. Huda noticed the pitcher on the nightstand and a full glass of juice next to it.

"Aren't you going to drink that, Dina?"

"Mom, you know I don't like juice."

Huda smiled. "I'll never forget how I used to trick you into drinking milk or juice when you were a little girl," she said. "But you're a grown-up now, Dina. Think of juice as medicine that'll help you get better faster."

"No way! I don't want to get better quickly. I'm very happy at home, with no school to worry about."

"Dina!"

Was her daughter saying that just to annoy her? Even though Huda was aware this might be the case, she couldn't control her irritation and said, "All children hate school, but it's an unavoidable evil. Once you're done, you can specialize in something you like."

"I like going to the movies, listening to rock music, going to the mall, and window-shopping. Can I specialize in those?"

Once again Huda felt her daughter had said that just to irritate her. She didn't answer and changed the subject instead. "Have your friends been visiting you?"

"Dad said they couldn't because I'm contagious. But I think he just wants me to rest."

"He's right," Huda said as she grabbed the glass of juice and held it close to Dina's mouth. "Please drink it. Not to get better—but just for me."

The girl looked at her mother, her lips pursed. Huda saw that look in her eyes—that same look that seven years hadn't been able to erase.

⸺ ⸺ "Hand me the big ones first," Dina had said. "Then we'll do the little ones."

It was the first holiday after Sharif had left us. Dina and I were decorating the little Christmas tree with colorful balls, silver ribbons, and tiny lights. Poinsettias stood in the corner of the room, and red and white candles decorated our tables. I carried the presents from my closets and started arranging them under the tree.

"I wish I still believed in Pâpâ Noêl," Dina said. She stood still in front of the tree and stared at me with sad eyes. Reprimand? Resentment? Both?

Should I ignore her comment or ask her why, even though I knew exactly what she wanted?

She didn't wait for my question. "I would ask him to bring Dad back to live with us."

I tried to make her feel better, to delude her into thinking our life was normal. "Dad's going to have dinner with us on Christmas Eve, and tomorrow we'll be with him and Grandma Umm Sharif," I said, trying to sound confident and cheerful. Dina didn't say anything, but was that sadness I saw? Reprimand? Resentment? All of those together? That look started in her eyes and spread out to the rest of her face. I looked away.

My parents came. Then when the doorbell rang at six, Dina ran to the door. "Dad! Dad!" I could hear her yelling from the kitchen as I checked the turkey in the oven.

"Where's Grandma Umm Sharif?" she asked.

"She has a cold, so she thought it would be better for her to stay at home. Here's your present from her. And this one's from me."

Presents are our way of making up for not being there and of showing our love, I thought to myself.

I heard my mother tell Dina, "Put them under the tree."

Then I went into the living room. "Hi, Sharif. Merry Christmas to you and your mother." For Dina, I put on a smile and a happy face.

Sharif responded with a smile (also for Dina?) and said, "Merry Christmas to you, too, all of you." He looked at my parents, having extended his greetings to them.

"Come on, Mom. Let's eat. I'm hungry."

"Are you hungry, or do you just want to open your presents?" I said to Dina. "Let's have a drink. The turkey's almost done."

Glad to busy myself instead of pretending, I went back to the kitchen to bring some nuts and drinks. Holidays brought families together, and here we were, together. Mom and Dad told stories about the holidays when I was a child. Sharif and I told the story of Dina and Pâpâ Noêl: how she had been scared of him, how she had yelled and run to Sharif, who had taken her in his arms and felt a warm fluid go through his sweater and shirt. "That's not Pâpâ Noêl. That's Papa Pee Pee!" he had said as he laughed and pushed her away from him. They talked, and I talked. They told their stories, and I told mine. They laughed, and I laughed. But inside me there was a gap, an emptiness that stories and laughter couldn't fill, no matter how hard I tried. Were the others feeling the same way? Were they trying to create a cheerful mood when there was nothing to be cheerful about? I looked at Dina stealthily. Was the little one feeling that lie, that fake happiness? She was busy devouring her food so she could open her presents. I couldn't see her eyes or figure out what was going on in her head, just as I never did after that—until that day of her ninth birthday arrived. The following holidays were a rerun of the first one, that first lie. What a lie that holidays have to be happy! We see friends and relatives, and we wish them "Happy Holidays." We decorate our houses and stores, wear new clothes, and send greeting cards. We give our families presents they don't want, but they pretend they do, and they give us presents we don't like, but we pretend they're exactly what we need for our happiness to be complete.

My father passed away and then my mother, but the "Happy Holidays" lie remained. Dina grew up and moved to her father and grandma's house. I went to their place now instead of their coming to mine, but the lie went on. As if meeting once or twice a year—faking love once or twice a year—was enough to bridge the gap of separation and erase those years of repulsion and differences.

That's what Dina's eyes protested that day. It was her ninth birthday. Every time her birthday came, those concerns became more pressing: Should I tell her she's going to move in with her father? Should I shake her little world with the idea of separation and change, or should I leave her content until it's time to do it? What if I keep her oblivious to her future? How fair will it be for her to find out suddenly that her life is going to be toppled once again? Will it be more fair to worry her before it's time? I felt these concerns every day, but they became more pressing each time we celebrated the fact that Dina was a year older—until Sharif put an end to my speculations.

Dina had come back from spending the day with him. As soon as I opened the door for her, she exploded. "Mom, is it true I'm moving to Dad's in two months? I'm not staying with you?"

I gently shut the door, took her coat, and hung it. I was trying to get over my surprise and gain some time before answering.

"Mom, is it true? Tell me!"

I made my voice sound soft and reassuring. "Honey, doesn't Dad deserve a chance to live with you, like I did? Dad loves you too."

"You promised you'd never leave me!" she yelled, tears spurting from her eyes as she ran to her room.

After all these years, she still remembered my promise! Could she understand and accept that the law in our country gives the father the right to custody? That those who make the law and implement it aren't mothers or children and don't care about how mothers and children feel? Especially the children. They live with their mother for a few years, and then, for reasons they don't and can't understand, they're taken away from the person who has nursed them since they were born and from the only house they've known, to a father they've only occasionally seen and a house that doesn't mean anything to them. Their childhood world is shaken. I followed Dina to her room. She was lying on her bed, her face buried in a pillow. Sobs shook her tiny body. I sat next to her and rubbed her head. She shook her head, moving it away from my hand.

"You don't love me. You lied to me!"

For kids, lying and loving are opposite things. She couldn't understand that lying and loving can be connected and that love is sometimes the only motive for lying.

"I do, Dina. I love you more than anybody else in the world. When I told you I wouldn't leave you, I wasn't lying, but the law's stronger than I am."

"What law?" she asked as she looked up at me with her tearful eyes.

I thought of a way to explain to a nine-year-old what "law" means. "People agree on some things they believe will lessen evil in our society and make it better," I explained. "We call these laws. For example, it's the law that puts a thief in prison so he doesn't steal again, hoping that the thief will regret it and there will be less robbery."

"And the law thinks that me staying with Dad is better than staying with you?" she asked. "How does it know? The law doesn't know me."

I couldn't help but smile. If only the law people had the logic of children! I didn't have an answer to her question, but I said, "I'll tell you a story I read in the paper. The court had implemented the law by ruling that a father got custody of his kids after divorcing their mother. The father was nasty, and he wouldn't let the mother see her children, so she missed them a lot. One day, when the father was at work, the mother went and took her kids."

"Bravo!"

"That's what you and I say, but the law says otherwise. The father went to the police and accused the mother of kidnapping his kids, so the police came and arrested her. They returned the kids to their father, and the mother is on trial now. She might be locked up for a couple of years, if not more."

"But she's their mother!" Dina's eyes were angry, disapproving.

"So if I refuse to let Dad take you, I'll be breaking the law."

"And they'll lock you up?"

"Dad isn't nasty. I'll be able to see you when you're at his place, just like he could see you when you lived here. I won't have to kidnap you."

"What if you broke the law and kept me with you? Would he lock you up?"

If I said no, she'd insist on staying, and if I said yes, I'd be lying. How would I know what Sharif would do? I said, "Dina, we have to obey the law, even if we don't like it."

"Why?"

"Because life would be a mess if everyone did as he pleased. Many times other people get hurt this way."

"But I'm not hurting anyone if I stay with you."

"What about your dad? Doesn't he deserve to have you live with him?"

"He's seeing me. Why does the law say he has to take me?"

I wanted to end our futile discussion, so I said, "When a large number of people decide to change the law, we'll be able to change it. You and I can't change it on our own."

"What about the mother who stole her kids?"

"No, not her, not us. There has to be a large number of people asking for the change. Now get up and go wash your face. Let's have dinner."

The following couple of months Dina would ask me every once in a while who'd take her to school when she moved to her father's, who'd bring her back home, if she could take her toys and books with her, if her friends could visit her, if Grandma Umm Sharif knew she liked chocolate cake so she could make it for her like I did.

"Mom, tell her I don't like milk and juice!"

I made her promises, answered her questions, and calmed her fears. Every question, every concern, big and small, tugged at my heart.

When her last summer vacation with me arrived, I wanted it to be the best one ever, something she'd never forget. I signed us up for a trip the university had organized for professors and their families for a small fee. When I arrived at the British embassy to get our visas, the employee took our applications, looked them over, and said, "Where's the girl's father?"

"At work."

"I can't give her a visa then. Her father has to be here."

"But I'm her mother!"

"It doesn't matter, ma'am. Her father has to turn in the application. He has to approve of her travel."

"She's traveling with me! Why wouldn't he approve?"

He didn't answer and gave me back the application. "Next," he told the person behind me.

It didn't matter to them that I was her mother and in charge of her. What if I had told him my husband had left me? So much for wanting a visa from a country that considered itself civilized and democratic. It had to apply my country's visa rules. I couldn't understand the logic of that law, anymore than Dina could when I tried explaining it to her.

"I don't want to have a birthday party!" Dina said when I asked her whom she wanted to invite to her ninth birthday. I wanted to plan the best party for her. Another "happy" occasion? She had finally refused that kind of happiness. I knew why, so I didn't ask.

"What do you want to do then?"

"Pack my stuff so I can go to Dad's." She looked at me with the defiance and resentment she had hid behind questions for two months. It had been building up in her young chest, and now it was exploding in the face of the adults whose logic she couldn't understand, but whose lies she did.

⁕ ⁕ Dina didn't tell her mother, "What have *you* done for me? Why should I do this for you?" but her look did—that same look that seven years hadn't been able to erase from Huda's memory. She put the glass of juice back on the nightstand and said gently, "The law also deprived me of you. It's not my fault." When Dina remained quiet, not looking at her, Huda continued, "When you get married, you'll see marriage is full of problems a woman can't solve alone . . . and sometimes the best solution is separation or divorce, unfortunately."

Dina finally looked at her mother. "It was the only solution for you?" Her question didn't conceal her sarcasm.

Huda said, "At the time, we thought it was the only one. Maybe we were wrong. I don't know. . . . *We* don't know. It's useless to go back. It's over. But don't you forget, Dina, that they took away my heart when they took you from me and that it's the woman who always pays the price, no matter what the reasons are. I'm telling you this because you're going to be a woman. You'll see."

"No matter what happens, I'd never give up my children!" Her eyes looked stern, defiant.

"I really hope, with all my heart, that you won't ever have to give them up. Not all marriages are bad, thank God. Uncle Halim and Auntie Sumaya are happily married. And not all bad marriages end in divorce. Many women put up with humiliation and deprivation and injustice or much worse so they don't lose their children."

"Unlike you!"

"Unlike me," Huda said coldly. She was quiet for a moment, then she said, "We'll see who you're going to support in the future. 'Counting slaps isn't like getting them.'"

And accepting them causes some more, Huda thought.

"So who's the one counting slaps?" Sharif asked from where he stood at the door. "And who's the one getting them?"

Huda didn't answer. It was her fight with Dina that had reminded her of the bitter past. She looked at her watch and said, "Since you're here, I better leave. I'll call in the morning to check on Dina." She kissed Dina and shook Sharif's hand.

"Say good-bye to your mother for me."

Then she left.

— 9 —

TEN DAYS LATER, Dina got better and went back to school.

"Do I pick you up on Friday so you can come sleep over?" Huda couldn't hide the excitement and hope in her voice. She could hear her heartbeats as she waited for her daughter's answer on the phone. Could their conversation on the first day Dina was sick have put her daughter off even more? She had visited her every day since, as soon as she was done with her lectures. Every day, Umm Sharif had received her with a long face and accusing eyes.

Sometimes she complained. "Her coughs kept me and her father up all night."

Huda knew her complaint wasn't really a complaint as much as it was blame for Huda's leaving her son.

Another time she said, "Dina's difficult. She won't take anything that'll help her get better."

"'Cause I'm happy at home!" Dina had said, laughing.

"You must have spoiled her when she was little," Sharif said.

She was always the one to blame for every mistake.

"She's always on the phone. As soon as her friends are back from school, the phone doesn't stop ringing."

Do you want her cut off from her world? Huda thought to herself. For her friends to forget her?

"Would you like me to take her to my place?" Huda said. "It's my duty to take care of her."

"So you can leave her by herself when you're at school?"

Of course, she was the selfish mother who neglected her daughter for the sake of her career! She saw the accusation in his eyes and heard it in his voice.

⸺ ⸺ That day, too, Dina had been sick when Sharif had come to pick her up. But that had been Dina the seven-year-old —not Dina the sixteen-year-old.

"Are you going to leave her at home and go to the university?" Sharif had asked then.

I saw the accusation in his eyes and heard it in his disapproving voice. It upset me that he actually thought I would do anything like that, so I decided to mock him.

"Dina's a big girl now, and she understands. She'll stay in bed and behave until I get back."

"That's impossible! I'm taking her. Mom's at home—"

"You told Grandma I'm sick?" Dina's voice interrupted him as she yelled to me from her room. "So she's coming tomorrow?"

I didn't look at Sharif. I walked ahead of him to Dina's room.

"Dad's here, Dina."

As soon as Sharif kissed her, she said, "Every time I get sick, Grandma comes over and tells me stories. That's why I like getting sick."

Sharif looked at me. I looked away. Even though he didn't say anything, I could imagine how angry and resentful he was.

⸺ ⸺ In her memory, all these images flashed by as Huda waited on the phone for Dina's answer. She knew Dina preferred not to come, that Dina wouldn't make the effort she wanted her to, preferring to spend the weekend with her friends, chatting, window-shopping, and listening to her modern music.

"Okay, Mom," she said. "I'll be waiting for you, as usual."

Huda's anxiety disappeared.

In front of the gate at school, Dina was lost in conversation with a boy who looked three or four years older. He had his arm around her. A few meters away Huda froze. No wonder Dina preferred not to spend the weekends with her. Was Rania's story repeating itself with her daughter this time?

That mother's despair over her pregnant daughter cut through the years. Did Sharif know who his daughter was hanging out with, whom she was with every time she went out, what she was really doing when she said she was at a friend's or at the movies? The fears raced, speeding around each other in her head. In the past, he had accused her of neglecting Dina, the child. Was he fully aware now of his responsibility toward Dina, the teenager? Should she confront Dina or talk to Sharif?

She approached her daughter. "Am I late, Dina?" She looked at the young man, who didn't change his posture or take his arm off her daughter. She thought of how different manners had become since her teenage years. She remembered her father's slap that day she was late instead of being home at six on the dot even though her father had known she was just at her cousin's.

Dina gently took her friend's arm off her shoulder. She said, "This is my friend Ramiz. He's in college."

Huda noticed the pride in her daughter's voice. Should she answer nicely? Coldly?

"Nice to meet you, Ramiz," she said, smiling. "What do you study?"

"Business management, so I can help run my dad's business."

A young man who seduced girls with his money. He had fun with them, with Dina, and then . . . ?

"Good luck," she said. "Are you ready, Dina?"

She grabbed her daughter's arm and pulled her to the car before she could get a chance to say good-bye to her friend.

"So, how did you meet him?" This was the first thing that came out of her mouth when she took off. She tried asking the question casually, as if she didn't care about the answer or even the whole issue.

"He used to go to my school," she said. "He was three years ahead of me, and we're still friends."

Huda looked at her daughter from the corner of her eye. Was it because she saw her regularly that she hadn't noticed her teenage daughter had turned into a young woman? She studied her face: she's a beautiful, young woman. A radiant face and wide, almond-shaped eyes above high cheekbones. Long, black hair in a ponytail, hanging over her thin, long neck. The same ponytail that Haifa used to proudly flip. Haifa, slim and tall, like Dina. Haifa who could wear a sack and pull it off well because of her great body. Haifa with her fair skin, clear face, and wavy blonde hair, also in a ponytail. Where had *she* ended up? For ten years, the only guy she had hung out with was Anis. "No wonder. He's rich!" the jealous ones said. Was it because he was rich? Maybe. Haifa had been shocked when she read in the paper that Anis had gotten engaged to his partner's daughter, who was also rich. He hadn't even bothered to tell her. Why would he? She was a toy, filling the void in his life until he started thinking about marriage. He married someone who suited his class, his family. And Haifa's youth was wasted!

Dina's fate wouldn't be like that! But Dina didn't live with her. Did Sharif know exactly what Dina was doing?

"Are we going to continue our tour in downtown Beirut, Mom?"

Dina's question crossed the wall of her fears and pushed them away. At least her daughter was hers for two days.

"If that's what you want. That's exactly what I'd like to do."

"Yeah, the weather's great."

"I could take pictures of some of the other buildings."

The girl turned to her mother and said, "Why do you take pictures of them? They're full of holes, and some of them are totally destroyed. They're ugly!"

Huda thought for a second. She said, "Dina, you love me. Today, I'm energetic and young. Are you going to stop loving me when I'm old and ugly?"

She glanced at her daughter before looking back at the road.

"Of course not, Mom. I love you because you're my mother, and you'll always be my mother . . . but you haven't answered my question."

"I did. Beirut is our city. We loved it when it was pretty. We lived and had fun in its downtown when it was full of life. Do you expect us to stop loving it now that it's abandoned, destroyed, and ugly?"

When Dina didn't say anything, Huda continued. "Plus, downtown is going to be completely different. These destroyed buildings won't be here forever. They'll be gone, and new ones will be built in their place. None of the landmarks we've known will remain, except those stuck in our memory or captured in the pictures we've taken. Memories fade after a while. Those who possess them die . . . but pictures remain."

"Who will they remain for? For those who didn't know these places?" Dina asked without hiding her sarcasm.

"They remain for those who have never lived through a vicious civil war. They'll be there to show them how man can destroy himself."

They had arrived home.

"Finally! We can take the elevator," Dina said, pressing the button.

Huda went into the kitchen to make dinner while Dina sat at her desk and started her homework so she could be ready for their tour the next day.

This time, Huda took her car and parked it on Fransa Street. They walked toward Bab-Idrees.

"Have these always been auto repair shops?" Dina asked as she studied the shops stretching out one after the other on both sides of the road. A car was being scrubbed here, another painted there, a third car's engine was being checked by a young laborer, a fourth had a guy lying under it.

"Of course not. That burned-down building used to be the Greek embassy, and that destroyed place next to it used to be our hangout when we were young," Huda said, pointing to a building thirty meters past the first one. "It used to be one of the most famous cafés for cake and ice cream. We'd come here on Saturdays and gorge on our favorite ice cream, *trois petits cochons*."

"Better than Scoozy or Bistro or the Chase?"

Who was taking Dina to these expensive cafés? Huda wondered.

Huda said, "All those places weren't there before the war. The Pâtisserie Suisse was the most famous one back then."

They crossed the street, went up to the wide open doors of the Coptic church. Huda stood at the threshold, unfolded her tripod and steadied the camera on it, adjusted the distance, lens, and flash, and started taking pictures: the cross and the drawings over the altar were unharmed, as were the statues of the Virgin and Saint Theresa. Huda turned the camera to take pictures of the two other saints who had lost their heads, the pockmarked pillars, and the other destroyed statues whose remains popped out of the niches. Dina stood contemplating the colorful glass windows that had survived.

Dina suddenly whispered, "Mom, look!"

A sparrow that had come in through the broken window flapped its wings. It began fluttering all over the church until finally perching on the head of one of the other statues that had survived over the main entrance.

"Whose statue is that?" Dina asked.

"Saint Louis," Huda whispered so she wouldn't scare off the little bird. "The church was established in his name."

She turned her camera, zooming in on the bird on the head of the statue.

"Is that why the bombs didn't get it?" Dina asked, smiling, as she watched the little bird, who, having found comfort at the saint's head, froze there. *Click. Click.* Huda took the picture before the bird could notice the two intruders who had disturbed the reverence of the silent church. Then it flapped its wings and left through the place where it had entered.

Huda carried the camera and Dina the tripod. They were on the side of the street where sewers ran and piles of trash filled gaps in buildings that hadn't been turned into garages.

"Do you want to take pictures of these too?" Dina asked, without hiding her disgust.

"No way! I want them gone. They weren't part of my past. Why would I want to remember or remind others of them?" Huda answered, irritated. "Unlike those." She pointed to a pile of rubble.

When they had reached Bab-Idrees, she continued. "This used to be the Ifranj market, where they sold the best vegetables, fruit, and cheese, and these arches, see their remains, were the first of the Jmil markets. They had small stores for sewing supplies, hats, and household goods."

Dina studied the scenery around her while Huda steadied her camera again. "What about the people who stayed here?" she asked. "Weren't they afraid of bombs?"

Huda followed her daughter's gaze: there was some laundry hanging on the balcony of a second-floor apartment in a half-dilapidated building. On another balcony that had lost its railing, two men were smoking a water pipe.

Before Huda could answer her daughter, a woman popped her head out and yelled, "Mohammad, come here right now!"

"I'll come when I'm done," said a teenager who was busy waxing a car.

"They weren't here, Dina," she explained. "All these buildings used to be offices, not residential houses. These people are war refugees who came here when the battles subsided. They came looking for shelter or work, as you can see."

They carried the camera and tripod and went down to Wagan Street.

"See these piles of rubble here. They're blocking what used to be the al-Tawila market, one of Beirut's most famous markets." My daughter is like a tourist, Huda thought. No, a stranger. A stranger in the city where she was born and raised.

"What kind of market was it?" Her daughter's question interrupted her thoughts.

"A fabric market, with things such as sewing supplies for dresses, as well as a market for shoes and purses."

"What's this?"

They had arrived at a small room with a dome. Dina stood and read out loud, "The corner of Ibn Iraq al-Dimashqi al-Shafi'y and al-Imam al-Ouza'y." She laughed. "What does a religious guy have to do with a fabric and dress market?"

"We didn't know this corner was here. It was hidden by the fabric and dress stores. When the bombs destroyed the stores, this humble corner became visible, and the believers renovated it." She kept quiet as she took pictures and looked at the humble corner before her. "As evidence that only the spirit endures in the face of man and time."

"What about the mosques and churches that were hit by bombs?" Dina asked. "Aren't those spiritual places, too?"

Her daughter's logic reminded her of the first thing she'd photographed that day, the Coptic church they'd left an hour ago. She didn't say anything.

After she turned off the camera and folded the tripod, she said, "Let's go see al-Ma'rad Street and the al-'Omari Mosque. Then we'll go home."

They went down from Bab-Idrees to the intersection of Wagan, Alemby, and al-Ma'rad and looked at the beautiful arches and the entrance of al-'Omari Mosque across from them.

Huda set up her camera and started taking pictures. "Thank God, they've started renovating the mosque's beautiful front," she said.

"What about the arches?" Dina asked.

"They'll be renovated, too, no doubt, because al-Ma'rad Street is the most beautiful street in downtown. In my opinion, at least."

"Why is it called "al-Ma'rad Street," Mom?"

"Because there was an exhibition here. That's how it got its name, and different stores remained there, in the lower half, on both sides of the street."

"And people lived on top?"

Huda didn't answer because she was busy steadying her camera and readjusting for distance and light. Dina thought her mother hadn't heard her, so she repeated her question.

"I never thought about these things, Dina. I know the offices and companies were on the top floors, but I do remember this part of the downtown didn't have any residential apartments. These apartments used to be banks, private offices, companies. People used to live in other parts of the downtown, Wadi Abu Jmil where we parked or Riyad al-Sulh Square. I remember going there with my mother to visit an elderly friend of hers when I was little."

Huda turned her camera to take more pictures while Dina stood silent, looking at the front of the mosque. Suddenly she asked, "How old is this mosque?"

"More than eighty years. Before that, it used to be a church that the Crusaders built over a Byzantine church, which, in turn, had been built over the remnants of a pagan temple."

"If they had left all the temples and old churches, downtown Beirut would have been a bunch of sacred places: temples, churches, and mosques."

"It would also have been a preservation of the beautiful architectural buildings. Next to the temples and churches that disappeared, there were other mosques that also disappeared as time went by." Huda was quiet for a moment, then said, "The places of worship aren't the only things that have disappeared."

Huda was very pleased that Dina was asking questions. She had succeeded in igniting her daughter's interest in history, her favorite subject, her specialization. Would it bring them closer? She put the camera in her bag and folded the tripod.

Did she dare ask? She hesitated then decided to take a chance. "Is Ramiz different than your other friends?"

They were heading back to the car on Fransa Street. Dina gave her mother a surprised look, but the mother noticed the slight blush that covered her daughter's adorable face.

"Why are you asking?"

Evading the question was an answer in itself, Huda thought.

"Because I saw you two lost in conversation." She hesitated, before adding, "and he had his arm around your shoulder."

Dina suddenly stopped and glared at her mother, "Mom, you don't just teach about the Middle Ages. You live in them."

Huda knew it would be useless to answer her, now at least. First, the girl needed to calm down. She decided to talk to Sharif and remind him of her former student Rania's tragedy and of their old friend Haifa's disappointment. She used to complain to her mother about the troubles of taking care of little Dina on her own: supervising her diet, her studies, and her entertainment; staying at home so Dina wouldn't be by herself; and having to ask her mother for help when Dina was sick. She smiled as her mother's response came back to her: "As a child gets bigger, my daughter, his worries get bigger with him."

She hadn't believed her then. But now?

— 10 —

SUNDAY AFTERNOON Huda dropped Dina off at her father's house. That same evening she called him.

"Sharif, I have to see you tomorrow. It's very important."

"I can't tomorrow," he said coldly. "I have a commitment."

He didn't ask what she wanted or why it was urgent.

"All right then, the day after tomorrow."

"I'm busy then as well."

So, what Sumaya had told her was true. At the time, Huda had responded, "Sharif is a free man." Still, she thought of her daughter. Did Dina know? Dina hadn't told her anything. Was it because she didn't know or because she didn't want Huda to know?

"Sharif, it's about Dina. I have to see you, please."

A moment of silence passed before his answer came. "Dina's perfectly fine. She was with you just a few hours ago."

She couldn't help raising her voice. "I don't know if she's going to stay perfectly fine. Please, Sharif!"

"Stay? What does that mean?"

Finally, he was showing some interest.

"I'll tell you when I see you the day after tomorrow. I'll be waiting for you in my office at four."

She hung up before waiting for his answer, before he could get a chance to put off meeting her. Was his new love life making him forget about his teenage daughter and his responsibilities toward her? And what about her, Huda? Wasn't she also free? She was a woman, though, and she had a daughter. She had a responsibility, too. The apple doesn't fall far from the tree. She wondered: Had she tolerated humiliation—her imprisonment at home—could there have been a chance that Sharif would come back to his senses and acknowledge his mistake and her innocence? Had she endured, for Dina's sake, would it have been logical for him to keep mistreating her? Wasn't he known for his honesty? Wasn't his name, "Sharif," perfect for him? Then there was his depression, which drove him to all that. Would she have been able to rid him of it? But what good had come from his trying to get rid of it himself? How had it affected him, her, and Dina? They both were responsible, but what about Dina? The morning sunlight broke its way between the blinds while the speculations were still running in her head.

Sharif entered her office at four on the dot. She was taken aback by his elegance, his refreshed face, his energy as he turned to shut the door, his graceful steps, which she had admired when he was young—and which he had lost for a while thanks to the years of failure and despair. It must be the elixir of love! Envy and deprivation pierced her heart as she stood to greet him.

"Have a seat, Sharif."

"So, what's the problem?"

He wanted to go back to *her* as soon as possible! Of course! Huda's feelings were now mixed with resentment.

"It's Dina," she said. "Sharif, do you know who she goes out with? Where she goes? What she does?"

She told him what she had seen the other day.

Sharif was silent for a while. "Should I be watching her every move? Spying on her every time she goes out?" he said. "Or are you saying I should forbid her from going out?"

Just like you forbade me, she wanted to say. But the result of that situation made her watch her tongue. "You can't stop her, but you can ask her," she said. "Try and find out what she's up to. Don't you remember what happened to my student, Rania?"

"Rania? What Rania?"

Was his new love making him forget details from the past, or did he want to erase everything of his past? She reminded him of Rania's tragedy.

"Dina's mature and rational," he said. "No guy can seduce her."

Was he saying that to free his conscience? Hadn't Rania, too, been mature and rational?

After a period of silence, Sharif said, "What do you suggest?"

"Ask her where she's going when she goes out. Follow her. Watch her from a distance, but don't let her know you're watching."

"So you are asking me to spy on my daughter?"

The disapproval in his question took her by surprise and got to her.

"Would you rather the girl go down the wrong path?" she said. "Plus, you wouldn't be spying. Just watching her for her own good." Or would you rather not sacrifice a minute of your time with *that* one? she added to herself. "Watch her two or three times only. If you are satisfied with what you see, you can leave her alone . . . until it's time to start watching her again from time to time."

Sharif didn't say anything. Wouldn't that be spying? Wouldn't it imply that he didn't trust Dina? What if Dina found out he didn't trust her and was spying on her? He'd lose her trust and her love. No way! What if Huda was right? He wasn't any less protective than Huda of his daughter's future, her life, and her happiness.

"What do you think, Sharif?"

"Honestly, I don't know. Imagine how Dina would react if she found out I don't believe or trust her."

Huda couldn't control herself any longer. "I wish you had thought of that so *I* didn't have to find out you didn't believe or trust me! Things would have—"

Her emotions choked up the rest of her sentence.

He answered calmly, "I see, *we* can see, where that got us, Huda. I don't want for that tragedy to be repeated with Dina."

Tragedy? So he regretted what happened? Why hadn't he expressed his regret earlier? Before it was too late? Was it too late now? What about the other one? Was he regretful for his own sake? Dina's?

"Dina's young, Sharif," she said. "She doesn't know what she's doing or what's good for her. She's going with the flow of her generation, the war generation."

⸺ ⸺ I looked at my watch: 3:00 A.M. I put my students' notebooks away and got up to shut the window. A car stopped in front of my apartment building. Curious, I popped my head out. Under the street lights, I saw a man step out of his car and open the passenger's door. Then a girl went out of the building. I leaned farther out. I couldn't believe it! It was Munia! At this hour? Where were her parents? I shut the window and checked up on Dina in her bed. Thank God, she was still a child.

The next day I met with the principal and told her what I'd seen. She sent for Munia. I looked at her in disbelief: her conservative blue school uniform; her chestnut braid hanging over her shoulder; her wide hazel eyes. All I could see was the innocence of her fourteen years.

"Can you tell your mother we want to meet with her?" the principal said firmly. Munia shifted her gaze from the principal to me and then back to the principal.

"What did I do?" she said. "I didn't do anything." Her tone of voice sounded like that of an innocent person who'd been accused of something. This must have upset the principal.

"You didn't do anything at school. What about outside school?" the principal asked, staring at her with piercing eyes.

The girl blushed, "What I do outside school is none of your business." Her boldness, her insolence, took us by surprise.

Trying to break the ice, I said, "Munia, you're a minor and our student. We are in charge of you—"

"In school only, not outside!"

"Inside and outside school! We don't want rotten students here, corrupting others," the principal said. "Anyway, I want you to bring your mother."

The girl insisted, "My mother trusts me. She knows everything. There's no need to send for her."

We didn't believe her, and I confronted her. "She knows you stay up all night with a male stranger?" I could tell by the way she looked that she was getting a little flustered. Had we embarrassed her?

"Since when is love a crime?" she said. "Bombing houses, blowing out countries, killing people . . . these are not crimes, or corruption? But love is?" There was anger in her eyes, her voice, her tiny shivering body.

The principal changed her tone of voice and said, "Bombing, destruction, and killing *are* crimes, Munia, but you're still young. You don't know what love is, true love. We don't want a man taking advantage of you. We don't want you confusing love with lust and becoming a victim. Just tell your mother to come here."

Suddenly the girl broke down, shaking with sobs. The principal and I looked at each other, baffled by what was going on. We waited a few minutes for Munia to settle down. The principal put her arms around Munia's tiny shoulders and gently told her, "Don't cry, Munia. Don't worry. We're going to sort this out with your mother. She loves you, and she's not going to hurt you. She just wants what's best for you."

"She's dead! A bomb killed her!"

It all became clear.

"Who are you staying with? Who's taking care of you and your little brother?" I asked, worried.

The girl was silent for a few minutes then said, "My grandma. My dad's away on business."

A grandmother couldn't—and shouldn't be expected to—look after a teenage girl. Meanwhile, a stranger was getting all the love that belonged to the absent father.

"Calm down, Munia. Go back to class. We'll see about this."

We decided to meet with her grandmother. We'd figure out how to free Munia from the fangs of that man, how to solve her problem. But what about the problem of others whom the war deprived of the love of a mother or a father—whom the barbaric war had deprived of the standards of good and evil, of ethics, and of the value of life? I asked myself those questions at that time, only to realize when I started teaching at the university how incapable I was of finding answers.

"Stealing is not a sin," a student of mine once said.

I had been shocked. "Not a sin? What kind of religion says it's not?"

"All religions that preach justice and charity and taking care of the weak and the poor," he said. "You should only rob rich people, those who've gotten rich by robbing others."

I looked at his worn shirt, his faded jeans. I couldn't convince him that rich people aren't all thieves and that thieves also rob people who aren't rich.

Another student had ordered Halim, "You have to change my grade so I can raise my grade point average and graduate."

When Halim had refused, the student had warned him, "You better change it. I'm not threatening you. A person who takes action doesn't threaten. He just acts." Then he had left Halim's office.

For weeks, Halim hadn't dared leave the university without Sumaya or one of our colleagues accompanying him, until he was sure the student's words were was just a threat—unlike Walid's. When Professor Ra'fat had refused to change Walid's grade, Walid had taken a gun out of his pocket, pointed it at the professor, put his finger on the trigger, and said, "Which one is more precious: your life or my grade?"

Ra'fat had been alone in his office.

When he had reached out for the phone, Walid had attacked him, causing the phone to fall to the floor, and yelled, "Don't move!" Then he had repeated, "So, your life or my grade?"

Ra'fat had changed his grade, left the university—left Lebanon. But Professor Fouad al-Rajeh couldn't leave, wasn't given the chance to leave. His body was found under a bridge. Who did it? Of course, we didn't know. Why? We didn't know that either. Maybe it was the war, the war generation. It was easy to say that, but it wasn't easy actually to accept it. As time passed, the question became more pressing: Are we going to be able to change it? How? When?

~~~ ~~~ Seated across from Huda, I remained silent.

I didn't believe her. I didn't trust her. Was I wrong? But where had my trust in Jawad gotten me? Jawad had sent me an agent to look at the land the factory had been built on so the agent could sell it for him. The land of my mother, who didn't even know that she didn't have it anymore. And Huda? Hadn't she pushed me into doing what I did, with her silent as well as verbal complaints? With her negligence? He shook off the anxieties of the past.

What should I do with my daughter? What should I tell her? Should I suggest that Huda talk to her? Dina lives with me, so she's my responsibility. Should I confront her? Watch her? Now, after I've let her do as she pleases? I've never asked who she goes out with or where. I've never thought things would end up this way. All I've ever cared about is gaining her approval, making her forget her mother's absence, showing her how much I loved her, and making her happy. I hadn't realized my little girl was no longer little, that she'd turned into a teenager. Has Aida distracted me? Aida has filled the void in my life and given me everything that Huda had deprived me of. When I marry Aida, Dina will have a normal family atmosphere. Aida will help me raise Dina. But will Dina accept that? She doesn't even know Aida exists. Have I known about Ramiz's existence? Dina and I live next to each other, not together. Huda sees her only twice a month, yet she's found out something I don't know, and I'm the one who sees her every day!

"What have you decided, Sharif?" Huda's voice interrupted his speculations and confusion.

"I haven't decided yet," he said. "I don't know. Let me think about it."

"Think about Dina's future, her life, Sharif."

When Sharif left, he was still immersed in his speculations and confusion. He got into his car and looked at his watch. Aida would be at home, and Dina would have gotten back from school. Should he consult Aida or talk to Dina? He headed home.

When his mother opened the door, he said, "Is Dina here?"

Why am I worried? he thought.

"Of course," his mother said. "Where else would she be? She's on the phone as usual."

Was she talking to *him*? Had she called him, or had he called her? He took off his coat and poked his head inside her door. Dina was sitting in a chair in front of the phone, her book open in her lap. She was listening attentively and writing something in her book every once in a while. A classmate must have been explaining a lesson she didn't get! It was Huda's fault. She had made him doubt his daughter. His dear, innocent daughter. If there was anything suspicious about her relationship with Ramiz, she wouldn't have waited with him for her mother or introduced him to her. She would have kept their relationship secret. No. He wasn't going to tell Dina anything that would turn her against him or make her feel he didn't trust her.

It felt as if a burden had been lifted off his shoulders.

━━ ━━ A week after he had visited Huda, she called him, "Have you confronted Dina? Have you talked to her?"

He couldn't explain it over the phone, and he didn't want to see her again. She wants me to doubt my daughter because I doubted her—to spoil my relationship with Dina, he thought.

He said calmly, "Since the last time I saw you, Dina hasn't left the house except to go to school."

"What about after school?" she asked. "Do you have any idea who meets her then? Ramiz was with her in front of the school gate!"

The panic in her voice exasperated him. Her paranoia about her daughter must have been a result of her own loneliness and deprivation. It gave him a sense of guilty pleasure.

"Dina's my responsibility, Huda. Don't worry."

"Your responsibility?" she yelled. "If you really knew your responsibility, you'd watch her, find out who her friends are, educate her. You wouldn't leave her—"

"If *you* had known your responsibilities, we wouldn't have gotten here! And speaking of education—"

The line went dead. Was he still using those years against her? Blaming her? She decided to confront Dina herself. Dina was her daughter—and her responsibility—too.

As usual, Dina was waiting for her in front of the school gate, but this time she was alone. Huda was relieved and bothered at the same time: How was she going to broach the subject? If she had found her with Ramiz, the same way they were last time, it would've been easier to confront her.

Dina got in beside her, kissed her, and asked, "So what are our plans for this Saturday?"

Was she making a mistake? Was her protectiveness toward Dina causing her to doubt her daughter for no good reason? Was she worrying unnecessarily? What about Rania's mother? Where had her trust in her daughter gotten her? And Haifa? Where had her trust in Anis gotten her?

"There's a group exhibition for Lebanese artists. We could go see it, if you like. And maybe see a play in the evening at the—"

"I don't like plays," Dina interrupted. "I can't sit there for two hours and watch people talk."

"Isn't that what you do at the movies, Dina?"

The answer came without hesitation. "Movies are different. Movies transport us from one place to another. There are different scenes, action, beautiful actresses, and cool outfits. They're easy to understand. You don't have to concentrate."

"Not all movies are like that, Dina."

"The movies I like are."

If this was how their conversation began, how was she supposed to talk to Dina about what she'd planned to talk to her about?

"You suggest, then, what you want us to do tomorrow, and I'll just say yes," she said. She wanted to win her over. Sharif had let her live as she pleased because he didn't want her to turn out like her mother. He hadn't tried to guide her. Or had that other one—whose news others were certain to tell me—kept him busy? Dina's vanity and her laziness weren't the issue now. Her behavior was. And her life. When should I confront her with what's been burdening me? Huda wondered. How should I start? What should I say? How should I do it without putting her off, stepping on her toes, and making her angry—without a misunderstanding or a falling out?

When they arrived home, Huda went into the kitchen to make dinner as usual while Dina did her homework. I'll let her finish her homework first, Huda thought, then I'll talk to her. She also decided that putting it off would give her more time to prepare what to say.

"Why don't you finish your homework, sweetie?" she told Dina when she started to help her clear the table and do the dishes.

"I just have my geography lesson left."

"Finish it, then."

Dina was surprised because her mother always insisted that Dina help her out in the kitchen after dinner so she would "be ready for married life." Her mother would say this jokingly. She went back to her room and books.

"Have you finished your homework?" Huda asked when Dina came out of her room and headed for the television.

"Yes, Mom."

"Let's not watch TV, Dina," she said. "I want to talk to you."

Dina gave her mother a puzzled look. Had she made her mother upset by refusing to go to the theater?

"It's okay, Mom. I'll go with you to the theater tomorrow."

Theater? Huda thought. What was she talking about?

Then she remembered and smiled. "No, it's not about the theater, Dina," she said. "Come here." She pointed to the seat next to her.

Dina approached her mother and sat down. She looked at her, still puzzled. "What's wrong, Mom?"

"Dina, you know how much I love you."

"Is that the problem?" she laughed.

Huda was silent for a moment. She said, "The problem is, I'm not sure you understand that all a mother cares about is her daughter's well-being."

"Of course I do." Her answer came quickly.

"Then listen to me," she said and told her the stories of her former student Rania and her old friend Haifa.

"What have I got to do with all that?" Dina asked before Huda had finished her last sentence.

"I don't want you to end up like them. To become—"

"I'm not stupid like your student Rania, and I'm not in love like your friend Haifa. Nobody can take advantage of me."

Huda hesitated before saying, "What about Ramiz?"

"Ramiz?" Dina laughed. "Ramiz? He's just a friend."

Huda wasn't convinced. "Just like any other friend?" she said. "That's not what it looked like when I saw you together."

"Mom!" Her voice was loud now. "Like I said, you still live in the ages that you teach about!" Then calmly, "Don't worry. Don't worry about me. I can take care of myself."

She got up from her seat and turned on the TV to let her mother know she was putting an end to their conversation. But she hadn't put an end to her mother's worries. Every teenage girl thinks she can take care of herself, that she's smarter than everybody else, and that she won't fall like the rest of them, Huda thought.

She decided to take matters into her own hands, but how could she convince Sharif? And Dina?

— 11 —

HUDA RAN TO THE PHONE that she'd heard ringing even before putting her key in the door.

"Hello? Huda?" The voice sounded familiar.

"Yes," Huda said. "Who is this?"

"Guess who? It's an old friend."

Who could it be? She knew the voice, but hadn't heard it in a while.

"Haifa?" Huda asked hesitantly.

"It's Najwa!"

"Najwa? When did you get back?"

"A week ago," she said. "You're the first one of all my old friends to get a phone call. How are you and Sharif? And Sumaya and Halim? Haifa and Anis? Did they get married? God, I miss you all so much!"

Her friend's questions crossed eighteen years of separation, reviving names and events that had become memories, and picking on wounds that hadn't become memories yet.

"We've got a lot of news, Najwa," she said. "Eighteen years worth of news! Why don't you come over? We'll have a cup of tea, and I'll tell you everything. How about you? How are you?"

"I'm back, for good. I also have a lot of news," she said. "A cup of tea sounds perfect. I'll be there at four. Will Sharif be there? By the way, how many children do you have, besides Dina?"

Huda ignored her first question. "Just Dina."

"Just one? How old is she now?"

"She's sixteen, Najwa. Yes, just one. If you had lived through the war we've lived through, you'd know why." Worried that Najwa might ask more questions, she said, "I'll see you at four then."

Huda went into the kitchen and set some teacups, sugar, milk, and a plate of cookies on a tray. Before her stood an image of Najwa, the hardworking, excellent student—Najwa, who had applied for a scholarship so she could go abroad and specialize. Had she done that merely because of her ambition?

⸺ ⸺ Jawad, Sumaya and Halim, Sharif and I, Najwa and Fouad. We had been inseparable. Halim and Sumaya got married so they'd never be away from each other. Sharif and I got married, thinking we'd never be away from each other. Fouad graduated the same time we did, even though he was older, because medicine took longer than humanities and law. The day he received his acceptance letter to do a residency at a hospital in New York, we all were thrilled.

"What are you going to specialize in?" we asked, excited and curious.

"Pediatrics. So I can treat your children."

Was he serious or just joking? We didn't dare ask, "What about Najwa?" because we knew specialization would take such a long time. Was he going to leave her? Would she go with him? How? He hadn't even suggested getting engaged. I watched Najwa. Was their impending separation spoiling her happiness? She seemed as happy for him as we were.

"She must really love him," I told Sumaya.

"She's just controlling herself, her emotions," Sumaya said.

"I got a scholarship to go study comparative literature," was the first thing Najwa told me when we ran into each other a month later. Sharif and I had found an apartment, and I was getting ready for our wedding. Education and its worries were worlds away from mine.

"Great!" I said, thinking of my appointment at the tailor's. I was running late. I said, "Congratulations! When are you leaving? I hope you can come to my wedding before you do."

"Of course I will," she said.

We went our separate ways.

A week after my wedding, she came to say good-bye. It was then that I remembered to ask her, "Where are you going?"

"New York. The scholarship left it up to me to decide where I want to go. I got accepted at Columbia."

So it wasn't just love or self-control, I told myself.

"You'll get to see Fouad!" I said. "Isn't that great?"

I was happy for her, with all my heart. I was glad she, just like Sumaya and me, wouldn't have to be away from her love. Who knows? They too might end up married, like we did.

Najwa left. In the first year, we got letters from her regularly. She told us about her studies, professors, new friends, and, of course, Fouad. She talked about the musicals, plays, and movies she saw.

"I'm not trying to make you envious. I'm just connecting you with the world out here," she'd write. We read her letters as we listened to the sound of shelling and the whistles of missiles. Then her letters stopped coming. She sent postcards for a couple of holidays. Later, even those stopped. The war hindered the mail service, just like it hindered us from thinking about anything outside our daily worries. The image of Najwa and Fouad disappeared from our minds.

⁓⁓ At four on the dot, the doorbell rang. Huda hurried to open the door for her friend. Long hugs. Warm kisses. Suppressed, happy tears at the reunion. Huda looked at Najwa's ring finger: there was no ring. She led her to the living room.

"First, tell me all about you and Sharif," Najwa said even before Huda could ask her about her life abroad or her plans in Lebanon. She briefly told Najwa the things others knew about Sharif's leaving her, Dina's living with him, and her job at the university with Halim.

"And you?" The absence of a ring made Huda limit her question to the "you" instead of asking about Fouad.

Najwa told her she had gotten her Ph.D. while the war was at its worst in Lebanon and that she had landed a teaching job at a university in Ohio.

"But my loneliness was killing me, and my homesickness," Najwa said. "I spoke in English all day. There were no Arabs I could talk to, open up to, in my own language. I'd walk on the street, a stranger among strangers. I didn't recognize a face, and no face recognized me. My country's troubles were mine alone. Nobody knew or cared about them. At night, I'd go to my apartment and sit in front of the phone, a great phone that never went out of service. It never rang either. I called no one, and no one called me. In the end, I just put it in a drawer so I didn't have to look at it, so it wouldn't remind me of my loneliness, my homesickness. Then I went to Washington, D.C., where I got a job at an Arab embassy."

"A job in your field?"

"No, of course not," she said. "But speaking and hearing Arabic was good enough for me. It was good enough to be reading the paper and writing letters in Arabic, and to be talking to people who knew what was going on in Lebanon and were distressed about it, even if it was just a facade."

"So you weren't lonely or homesick anymore?" Huda asked and got up. "Excuse me, one second, Najwa. Let me put some water on the stove."

"I'll come with you."

She followed her to the kitchen. Huda filled the kettle with water, lit the stove, and put the kettle on it.

After a period of silence, Najwa said, "I may not have been lonely anymore, but I was still homesick. I met some Arabs, and through them and my work I met some non-Arabs too. I got invited to parties and dinners. Not to mention that the Kennedy Center in D.C. always booked the best musicians—"

"So," Huda interrupted, "your life was rich, socially and culturally."

The water was boiling. Huda turned off the stove and poured some water in a teapot. She carried the tray into the living room. Najwa followed her without commenting on what she'd said.

"Would you like some sugar? Milk?" Huda asked.

"Just milk, please. No sugar."

Each of them grabbed a cup of tea and went back to their seats. Najwa took a sip and said, "It was socially and culturally rich, but it was empty."

"What more could you ask for, Najwa?" Huda said. Fouad's love? His presence?

"Friends, parties, and invitations don't take away loneliness and homesickness, Huda. Maybe they made me feel that way even more. I met people who had known each other for years. At gatherings, they'd talk about their memories, often of their childhood or school days. I listened and laughed with them, but like an outsider would, behind the wall of the past that separated me from them." She went back to her cup, silently sipping her tea.

Huda hadn't dared mention Fouad yet. She said, "Didn't you run into any of your old acquaintances? Isn't the United States full of Lebanese who left during the war or even before—especially in a place like D.C.?"

For a second, Najwa's lips arched into a slight smile, which then disappeared. She grabbed a cookie from the plate Huda extended to her. "I did, Huda, but the ones I met wanted to forget the past, close the book on Lebanon, so they could excuse themselves for leaving their burning country and for abandoning ship. Perhaps they did it to erase whatever it is that made them feel guilty or hurt them. They forgot or pretended to have forgotten that, for them, Lebanon was like a lemon they had squeezed dry and then thrown away. I don't know. Perhaps they wanted to adjust to their new environment and become well integrated. Perhaps they were right. What's the point of living in the past and longing for it when there's no going back?"

"But you did come back, Najwa, and others did too."

They put their cups back on the tray.

Najwa said, "It's because some people, and I'm one of them, couldn't do otherwise, for different reasons. Most of them couldn't get jobs."

Huda wondered if she should ask Najwa why she had come back even though she did have a job.

As if reading Huda's silent question, Najwa said, "When I was living in D.C, I didn't feel fulfilled with my job. It was futile, and its only advantage was paying the bills. So I went back to New York."

To Fouad? Huda wondered. She extended the cookie plate again.

"No, thanks," Najwa said. "I started working for a committee for the defense of Arab artists' freedom, their freedom of speech, writing, publishing, and artistic expression. Remember, literature is my specialty."

"Why did you come back then?"

"Because I felt I could do more here."

"Defending rights?" Huda asked, sarcasm rich in her voice, her smile. She remembered Qasim's disappearance, Khalil's back, Professor Ra'fat's immigration, and Professor Fouad al-Rajeh's corpse.

"That, among other things," Najwa said. "I can also teach and contribute to social and humanitarian causes, things our country badly needs."

Huda picked up the tray and carried it to the kitchen. She wanted to give herself more time before asking her friend the question that had been on her mind since she had heard her voice on the phone. When she came back into the living room, she saw Najwa looking at a picture of Dina on the shelf near the desk.

"This is Dina, right?"

"Yes, that's her," she said, "but it's an old picture I took almost a year ago. She's changed a lot since then. She's a young woman now."

"She looks really pretty."

Unfortunately, Huda thought.

"So, how's Fouad? Didn't you see him when you went back to New York?" She didn't want to say, "and before you left New York," because she was afraid she'd be picking on a wound she was certain was still there, even if it seemed to have healed—which Najwa's slight blush and anxious look confirmed.

"Our relationship ended a year after I got there." She was silent for a moment. She said, "I can't blame him, Huda. Maybe he did love me, but not as much as I loved him. Otherwise, he wouldn't have let me go."

"Why? How?" Huda said, encouraging her friend to go on.

"The war in Lebanon was getting more violent and complicated, and we realized we couldn't come back, not in the near future at least." Fouad thought about his future and the fact that he couldn't practice medicine in the United States because he wasn't American, so . . . "

"He looked for someone who'd give him the citizenship," Huda finished for her. "He married an American, right?"

"Exactly. He didn't stay in New York, and he got a job at a hospital in South Carolina. I found that out from a friend of his when I went back to New York."

"So Fouad joined the thousands of educated people we've lost," Huda said sadly.

"Thousands of other fresh graduates will take their place, like your students and other students."

As soon as Najwa gets a job, she'll become acquainted with those "fresh graduates," Huda thought. She remembered Dina.

"I haven't asked you about our other friends," Najwa said. "How are Sumaya and Halim, Haifa and Anis, and Jawad?"

"Sumaya and Halim are fine. I barely see anybody except for them, especially since Halim is my colleague at the university."

"And their kids?"

"Unfortunately, they couldn't have children. I don't understand how Sumaya fills the void in her life without a child or a job to keep her busy."

"You want to go visit her and fill some of that void?" Najwa asked, laughing.

"Sure," Huda said. "And as for Haifa, she's in Paris, as far as I know," and told her everything she knew about their old friend.

"What about Jawad?"

Huda hesitated and thought about it for a while. "We don't see him anymore," she said. "Sharif needed some financial help, and Jawad refused to lend him any money unless Sharif registered his mother's land in Jawad's name."

"What's wrong with that? Jawad had to have some sort of guarantee in case Sharif couldn't pay back his debt."

Huda didn't want to talk about the real reason behind the two men's estrangement. She said, "Sharif expected his friend to help him out for nothing in return. He believed the proverb, 'A friend in need is a friend indeed.' Maybe it was a mistake. Anyway, when Sharif couldn't pay off his debt and lost his land, he got mad, and they had a falling out."

"So," Huda said, changing the subject, "when do you want to go visit Sumaya?"

They set a date for the following afternoon.

— 12 —

MAY. SUMMER WAS AT THE DOOR. Huda was in the dressing room trying on a blouse she had picked to go with her floral skirt.

"How do you like this dress?" It was Dina's voice! Huda's arm froze, outside of the sleeve. Who was Dina talking to?

"I don't like the color. I like dark colors."

Huda finished putting on the blouse quickly, straightened out her skirt, and slid open the curtains of the dressing room. Dina was with Ramiz! They were busy looking at the dresses, so they didn't see her. Dina was actually getting his opinion on her outfits. Was he just a friend?

"Don't worry about it. I've been keeping an eye on her," Sharif had told me when I asked him to be more vigilant with Dina.

"You may be keeping an eye on her," I said. "But I'm her mother. I can talk to her about certain things, and she can open up to me about things she may not share with a man, even her father. Why don't you let her live with me, Sharif?"

"No way!" he said without even giving my suggestion any thought. "You're no more protective of her than I am."

I couldn't understand why he insisted that Dina stay with him now that he'd found someone to love. Did he want to hurt me, get back at me, even after all these years?

I decided to use my last weapon. "I'm not more protective, but I'm less occupied with someone else!"

That was how Sharif found out I knew about his other woman. I hadn't cared about the gossip people shared with me about him. I was always saying, "He's a free man. Our relationship is over." But now?

"My personal life isn't any of your business!" he yelled. "I'm free."

"You're free with your own business, not your daughter's!" I yelled in turn. "I'm not going to let Dina become a victim of your freedom and negligence!"

"I haven't been neglecting her," he said without lowering his voice. "She's nobody's victim. She knows there's no one else in my life." Then, in a calmer tone, "Go ahead and ask her. Ask her if she wants to live with you."

He told me to do that because he knew what Dina's answer would be, just as I did. Dina knew I wouldn't let her do as she pleased, that I wouldn't let her get carried away in her superficial fun. How could I convince her? She didn't know that there was another love in her father's life. I was afraid if I told her, her seemingly unshakeable world would collapse over her head. She was torn from me when she was still a child, and now she would be torn from her father. Then again, it was her future, her life, that was at stake! I waited until she came over for the weekend.

"What do you think about moving in with me, Dina?"

My question took her by surprise. "And leave Dad?" she said. "Why?"

I had thought about it carefully, so I calmly said, "Because I'm alone, and your dad lives with his mother."

"You've been alone for ten years. Why haven't you thought about taking me before?" was her logical reply.

"Dina, remember when you were little and didn't want to leave me, I told you the law forced me to give you up. We hated the law then, you and I, and it wasn't—"

"Has the law changed?" she interrupted me. Was she being sarcastic?

"Unfortunately, no. It hasn't changed. But you're older now, and I think you have the right to choose."

I studied her face, looking for traces of hesitation, a ray of hope. She lowered her eyes, thinking. The fact that she was thinking about it meant she wasn't already set on saying no. I became hopeful.

"No," she said, "I'm not going to leave Dad. He doesn't love Grandma Umm Sharif as much as he loves me."

"What about me, Dina? Don't I love you?"

She was silent for a few minutes, then said, "You do love me, Mom, but you don't understand me like Dad does. I grew up at Dad's, and he knows me better. He knows what I like and don't like."

Her words stabbed me. Did she believe he knew her just because he let her do as she pleased while I didn't? Then I remembered: when I was her age, I used to think the same way—that my mother wouldn't let me have everything I wanted and was critical of my behavior because she didn't understand me.

"That's what I used to tell my mother when I was your age, but she—"

"You were living with her," Dina interrupted firmly. "She was supposed to understand you, but I don't live with you. You don't know me well."

I know more than you think, my dear, I said to myself. "If you live with me, it'll be my chance to get to know you better and for you to get to know me better. What do you think?"

She was firm in her refusal.

⸺ ⸺ Huda froze in front of the mirror, watching the people behind her.

"Do you like it, ma'am?" the clerk's question pulled her out of her preoccupation.

"Yes, I do. How much is it?" she asked loud enough for Dina to hear her.

"Mom!" Dina said. She hurried toward her.

Huda pretended she was surprised to see her. "Dina! What are you doing here?"

"I'm picking out a dress." Noticing her mother's questioning eyes shift between her and Ramiz, Dina added, "I like Ramiz's taste, so I like getting his opinion."

The young man came closer and extended his hand to Huda. She couldn't tell him she was happy to see him again because she wasn't, and she couldn't criticize Dina's behavior in front of him, even though she wanted to. She extended her hand, out of courtesy, but without saying anything.

Perhaps she didn't ask for my opinion because she thinks I live in the Middle Ages. But why was she consulting this stranger? When she looked at Dina, she saw Haifa's face instead—but now with gentle wrinkles around the corners of her mouth and blue eyes that had lost their luster.

Huda shook off this image of her friend and asked, "Would you mind, Dina, if I also help you choose?"

"Not at all, Mom."

Huda couldn't tell if her daughter had agreed out of politeness or embarrassment or because she really wanted her mother's advice.

She decided to do things differently as far as Sharif and Dina were concerned.

⸺ ⸺ As usual, she picked Dina up to spend the weekend at her place and let her finish her homework on Friday evening.

The next morning Dina asked her the usual question. "What are we doing today?"

This time, Huda said, "We're going to talk."

Surprised, Dina said "Just talk?"

Trying to sound warm, Huda said in a calm voice, "When I suggested you live with me two weeks ago, I didn't tell you the real reason for my request."

She could tell her daughter was getting anxious. She continued, "Your dad loves you very much. It's true. I also love you very much. But Dad loves someone else as well, and I don't. There's no—"

"Dad doesn't love Grandma Umm Sharif as much as he loves me!" she interrupted. "I've already told you that!"

"I'm not talking about Grandma Umm Sharif. I'm talking another woman, Dina."

"That's a lie!" she yelled in her mother's face and looked at her with angry, protesting eyes. "That's not true!"

Huda kept quiet for a few minutes so her daughter could regain her composure. Then she continued in the same warm tone. "I tried keeping it from you, just as your father did, but I'm afraid there will come a day when he can't be without her because he needs a wife to be his companion and to take care of him. Also, this woman isn't going to stay in a relationship with a man who won't marry her. So they are going to get married, and you're going to become a victim."

When Dina didn't comment, Huda continued. "He can find a thousand ways to outsmart the church laws and get a divorce. If not, he can always become a Muslim. Anyway, all religions are fundamentally the same. It doesn't matter if a person is Muslim or Christian, so—"

This time Dina interrupted her. "You could get married, too, if Dad gets a divorce."

Huda smiled. "It's not the same for a woman in her forties, not in our country at least," she said. "Many men get married, even for the first time, when they're older than forty-five, but it's very rare for a single woman in her thirties to find someone who wants to marry her. And if she's divorced, it's almost impossible. I've always thought of that, Dina. This is probably the main reason why courts in the West grant the woman, not the man, the right of custody, because the mother will most probably be there for her children, but the father won't."

She grew quiet for a second, laughed, then continued. "Anyway, my dear, I'm not thinking about getting married at all. Nobody loves me, and I don't love anybody. I'm yours alone and always will be."

Dina had lowered her eyes and put her head down, and Huda didn't want to disturb her thoughts.

She couldn't tell how long they had been silent before Dina said in a sad, low voice without lifting her head, "I've noticed Dad's been paying more attention to what he wears. I'm so stupid. I thought I was the reason because I'd told him I was impressed by Ramiz, more than anybody, because of his stylish clothes. I thought Dad became stylish to impress me."

"That doesn't mean he doesn't want to impress you, too, Dina." Was she trying to lessen the impact of her daughter's shock? "Think carefully about what I told you. My house is your house, and my salary is enough for me and you. You can see your dad whenever you want. Now, why don't you help me make lunch so we can go shopping in the afternoon? I want you to help me pick out a present for Auntie Sumaya. It's her birthday."

— 13 —

NAJWA HADN'T MISSED a single employment ad. For three months, she'd been buying different papers, filling out dozens of applications, and making dozens of phone calls. All of it was useless.

"The country's going through an economic crisis," her mother said.

"Just be patient," her sister said, trying to encourage her. "Things'll start looking up for you."

"People won't hire you if they don't know you personally or at least know someone who does," her brother-in-law finally confirmed. So she contacted some of her friends and acquaintances, and sure enough, something came up.

"I know someone who owns a publishing house and is interested in publishing works translated from English or French. I told him about you. Here," Halim said, handing her a piece of paper with the man's address and phone number.

Najwa called and made an appointment, grabbed her resume, and left.

"I'd like you to translate this book for me," said Mr. Hannoum, handing her a volume by an English writer on Japanese civilization and its progress in the modern age. Najwa glanced at a page in the middle of the book: technical jargon and dense style that would require finding the right equivalents in Arabic.

"How much do you need to translate it?" Mr. Hannoum's question interrupted her thoughts.

"It's a hard book. It'll take time, I—"

"I'm not talking about time only. Time and money."

Najwa thought for a while, the man silently looking at her. She said, "It's seven hundred pages. It'll take me at least seven or eight months."

"Eight months!" he yelled in her face. "You're going to be translating this book, ma'am, not writing it."

He stood up, walked to the bookshelf on his left, and pulled out a book. He handed it to her. "This book is no smaller than the one on Japanese civilization. It was translated in less than three months and for a thousand dollars. The translator is a graduate of one of our best universities!"

Najwa realized this man's standards were different than hers, but she grabbed the book, opened it, leafed through it, and read a random page. She read a sentence from the first paragraph; she didn't get it. The sentence was long, so she reread it carefully. Slowly. What was the meaning of all that? She looked at the title of the book again. Under the title, it said, "Translated from French." She read the sentence for the third time, this time literally translating it into French. Finally, she got it, and smiled. Not only was the translation meaningless, but in some places in the book it was saying the opposite of what the original author must have intended.

She gave Mr. Hannoum his book back. "I'm sorry, sir. My translation would be nothing like this. Plus, I can't translate such a big, difficult book for only a thousand dollars."

He grabbed the book with shaking hands. They and the look in his eyes told her he was angry, but he also raised his voice. "This is one of the best translators! And this book has been very popular everywhere in the Arab world. I wouldn't be able to sell it for a reasonable price if I paid more for its translation."

He stood up; their meeting was over.

You haven't even paid anything for translation rights, Najwa thought to herself as she stood to shake the man's hand on her way out.

"A graduate of one of our best universities . . . one of the best translators" kept ringing in her head as she headed for a cab to go back home. She felt exactly as she had felt when she had arrived for her appointment: disappointed. "One of the best translators," she repeated to herself. That's what Mr. Hannoum claimed in order to promote his business and beat my price before I even named it. Najwa felt depressed: Was that the kind of book that people who read only Arabic were reading? These books corrupted their language, regardless of the translations' distortion of the original meaning, if they made any sense at all.

"Did you get it?"

She was met by her mother's restless question. Najwa felt ashamed. What should she tell her mother, who had always been proud of her outstanding daughter?

"I can't accept the kind of money they've offered, Mom."

"Isn't it better than nothing?" was the predictable reply.

Her mother couldn't understand that her pride, qualifications, and experience wouldn't allow her to accept what they had offered and that she didn't want to be considered one of those "other translators."

"I'd rather spend my time looking for a more satisfying job."

Her mother looked at her with reproach and disappointment. "Our neighbor, Talal, found a job as soon as he graduated, and he wasn't outstanding like you. He didn't have your kind of degrees either."

"Maybe that's my problem, Mom, degrees and experience that this country doesn't need, not now at least," she said. "Or maybe I just haven't found someone who does need them. Don't worry. I'll keep looking. There must be something for me out there."

"Why don't you wait until April or May?" Huda advised Najwa when she came over to update her on the job hunt. "By the end of the academic year, schools will know what teachers they'll be needing."

"Do schools need Ph.D.s?" Najwa asked. She didn't want to add: Wouldn't universities be in greater need for my degrees?

As if reading Najwa's thoughts, Huda said, "Of course, with your degrees you should be teaching at a university. Not to mention that professors get paid more than schoolteachers. But there are more schools than universities, and they're always looking for new teachers."

"But aren't universities also looking for professors to replace those who left during the war?"

It was a logical question for someone who had lived abroad for years, so Huda explained, "Because of the war, a number of professors joined the university, and not all of them were qualified. Some were hired as a result of political pressures, and some for lack of better professors. Anyway, it's very hard to fire them now. Whoever stayed in the country, such as these people and myself, has taken advantage of the situation." She smiled at her friend.

"You mean whoever had the privilege of going abroad for specialization during the war and of getting away from the terror and death has to pay the price for that now?" Najwa couldn't hide her frustration.

"I don't mean that at all, Najwa. I'm just trying to tell you how things really are, things you may not be aware of."

"What about the standards for students and the future of this country? Nobody cares about those?" Najwa asked. She thought of the book translated by "one of our best translators, a graduate of one of our best universities."

Huda was upset by Najwa's question. "Did the people who left the country think about those things? We, those of us who stayed here, tried with our little resources to make sure the schools and universities were still running at least. We tried preserving the country's present, but its future we haven't had the luxury to think about. Maybe those who have forgotten the past and renounced the present can do something about the future."

Huda's sarcasm hit home, and Najwa didn't answer. After a few minutes of silence, Huda said calmly, consoling her friend, "Any country that's been through seventeen years of war is bound to face endless problems, Najwa. The deterioration in the standards of students and professors is just one of them, and it's a result of other problems. The important thing now is that we start improving things, but acknowledge that it's going to take years. Now, let's go make some tea. I'll call the school where I used to teach. I'll introduce you to the principal in case they have any vacancies for next year. Plus, Najwa, I honestly think it's more important to improve the quality of our schools because they are the foundations for university. It's very hard, if not impossible, for us to improve the quality of universities whose students have spent months in bomb shelters throughout the past seventeen years. Let's prepare better students for the future."

They went into the kitchen. While Huda was filling the teapot with water, Najwa asked, "How are things with Dina?"

Huda turned on the stove and put on the teapot. "I'm going to try and get her back. I'm so worried she's headed down the wrong path. Sharif lets her live as she pleases, especially now that his new love is keeping him busy."

"New love? Who is she? Since when?" Najwa's curiosity kept the questions flowing from of her mouth.

"I don't know, Najwa," Huda said. "For more than a year now, my friends and acquaintances have been telling me they always see him with a woman.

They haven't kept it from me that she's younger, of course, and that she's an attractive and elegant woman. How true these things are, I don't know. They say it with a kind of pleasure. I know well they're indirectly blaming me for his leaving me. They're trying to make me feel envious and regretful. After all these years, I don't feel anything toward Sharif and just see him as my daughter's father."

"That's unbelievable, Huda. What about your love? We all know how much you two were in love."

Because you're still in love with Fouad? Huda thought. On the screen of her memory, her last years with Sharif flashed by: his depression, reproach, humiliation, and accusations, the religious court.

"There are things love can't survive," Huda said in a sad tone. Then, in a different tone, "Right now my daughter is the only thing on my mind. She's at a dangerous age and needs to be closely watched, and I think Sharif is too busy to do that."

The water started to boil. Huda poured some of it into the teapot, put in a spoonful of tea leaves, and added some boiling water. She carried the teapot and cups to the living room. Her preoccupation with making tea saved her from continuing a conversation she preferred not to pursue.

— 14 —

WHEN DINA GOT HOME FROM SCHOOL at three, she was relieved that her father was, as usual, there.

"Dad, you want to have a snack with me?" she asked after putting her books in her room.

Sharif looked at his watch. "I'll sit with you for fifteen minutes," he said. "After that, I have an appointment."

She turned her back on him and went into the kitchen so he couldn't see she was upset. He has an appointment every day, she thought. I can't talk to him for half an hour because of his appointments. Everything Mom said must be true.

She heard his footsteps.

"Where's Grandma?" she asked, taking out a bottle of Pepsi and some cake from the fridge.

"She has a dentist's appointment. She won't be late."

"Do you want a piece of cake?" she asked without looking at him.

"No thanks. I already told you, Dina, I have to leave in fifteen minutes."

She opened her Pepsi, cut a slice of cake for herself, and put the cake back in the fridge. Without saying a word, she sat down and started eating. Sharif sat across from her.

"How was your day, sweetie?"

She kept looking at her plate as she cut a bite of cake. "Like any other day." She took a gulp of her Pepsi.

"That's not what it sounds like," he said. "You're upset. What happened, Dina?"

"Nothing. Who says I'm upset?" She didn't lift her eyes from the plate as she cut another bite.

Sharif looked at his watch again. He couldn't be late for his appointment because of a moody teenager. He stood up and bent over to kiss her forehead. "I'll leave you then. Study well."

Dina waited until he had shut the door, then got up from her seat and looked out the window. After seeing her father get into his car, she ran to her room. She pulled her suitcase off the top of her dresser, packed some clothes and shoes, grabbed the books on her desk, and quickly left the house. Then she hailed a taxi and disappeared.

When Sharif got home at nine, his mother opened the door before he reached it. She asked, "Is Dina with you?"

The worry in her voice took him by surprise. "With me? No. She was home when I left."

"I didn't find her when I got back, so I thought maybe she was with you."

Sharif went to his daughter's room right away: her books were gone. Could she be studying at a friend's? This late? Who?

"Have you called her mother?" he asked.

"I tried several times, but I couldn't get through."

"Maybe she's trying to call to let us know she's there. I'm going to check if she's at Huda's."

He hurried out, started up his car, and headed to his former home.

"Sharif, I don't know what to do. Rula isn't back from school."

I could hear the fear in As'ad's voice that night. I looked at my watch. "It's nine, and she hasn't been back?"

"We called the school. We called her friends. Nobody's seen her."

"Have you called the police?"

As'ad hesitated. "I was worried. We didn't want her name on record at the police station."

"You're worried about a police record, but you're not worried her life may be in danger?" I couldn't help yelling into the receiver. "I'm coming right now."

At the time, I had thanked God that Dina was still a child and that she didn't have to go to school and come back alone. Granted, the shelling had stopped for months, but armed men were still out there. There were plenty of shady characters, and Rula was a beautiful young woman. Could she have been attacked? Was her body now trashed somewhere like the girl they found in the woods a week ago and couldn't identify? I shuddered. "If this war had taken place in any other country, so many more people would have been victims of rape and crime," As'ad had said that day about the news we had just read in the paper. Would he be saying the same thing now that his daughter had disappeared? Thoughts raced in my head as I sped to his house.

The entire house was lit up. A clamor of voices reached me when I was still on the sidewalk. I hurried up the stairs.

"Have you heard anything?" I asked.

The house was crowded. The voices hushed, as people stared at me.

"Nothing," As'ad said. His wife was sitting away from him, her face buried in her hands, her body shivering with silent sobs.

"Let's contact the police then!" I said, grabbing As'ad's arm so he wouldn't have a chance to hesitate.

The police station wasn't far. The officer in charge took down the girl's name, her ID number, her personal description, her address, and the details regarding the last time anyone had seen her.

"You're saying she's a beautiful girl?" he asked. "Could she have eloped with a groom you didn't approve of?" The policeman gave As'ad a sleazy smile. I wanted to slap him.

The devastated father said defensively, "My daughter's only seventeen, sir. There's no groom to approve or disapprove of."

I felt bad about making him go to the police, who covered their impotence with sleazy jokes. We left.

I called Mom and told her I wasn't going to leave As'ad. The house gradually emptied except for Zahi and his wife, As'ad's family, and myself. We stayed up all night, drank one coffeepot after another, our eyes fixed on the phone—a phone whose silence confirmed our fears. Every once in a while As'ad would go out to the balcony, look at the street for a few minutes, and come back in, disappointed. The crowing of the roosters announced the crack of dawn, then the light of the early morning made its way into the room, sun rays dazing our exhausted eyes. Suddenly, there was a loud thumping at the door. As'ad jumped from his seat and opened it. A priest stood before him.

Our hearts almost stopped. The priest looked at the ID in his hand and asked, "Is this Mr. As'ad Damaj's house?"

"I'm As'ad." He stared at the ID in the priest's hand. I was next to him, so I reached out for it and saw that it was Rula's. The blood in my veins froze. I handed the ID to As'ad.

"Where did you find it?" As'ad's question came as if from the heart of an abyss. Munia had hurried toward us with Zahi and his wife.

"Come with me," the priest said and turned his back.

"Stay with the kids," As'ad told Munia. As'ad, Zahi, and I ran after the priest.

"Where did you find my daughter's ID?" As'ad repeated between broken gasps as we got in the priest's car.

"In a jacket on a seat in the church. I found it when I went in to prepare for mass."

"What about Rula?" were the only words that came out of As'ad's mouth.

"There was nobody in the church," he said. "I found the jacket on a bench, so I went through the pockets to see if I could find out who it belonged to. That's how I found this ID. Fortunately, there was also an envelope with your address on it."

When we reached the highway, the priest headed north. It was only then that it occurred to As'ad to ask, "What church was it?"

"A church in Byblos."

"Byblos?" we asked at the same time. What had taken her to Byblos? I thought of the news of that girl's mysterious disappearance and of her corpse in the woods of the al-Fanar.

I sneaked a look at As'ad. He had turned his face toward the priest next to him, but I could see how his cheeks seemed drained of all blood, the only color in his face coming from the terrified, bloodshot eyes fixed on the priest. None of us said a word. Finally the car entered the city of Byblos and took a left toward the sea. Before stopping, we saw from a distance a girl walking quickly on the beach. The priest stopped his car in front of the church, and we got out. We stood in place there, staring at the faraway girl. Was it curiosity? No, hope. She suddenly turned around and without slowing down headed back in our direction.

"Rula!" As'ad yelled as we ran toward her. She kept walking, her head down. When we got a bit closer, she felt our presence and lifted her head for a second, then turned around and started running in the opposite direction.

"Rula, sweetheart! It's me, Dad!"

She froze in her place and slowly turned toward us. As soon as we reached her, she ran into her father's arms without a word, a sound. As'ad pulled her close to him, and we stood watching her: disheveled hair, torn clothes, scratches and dried blood on her bare legs. The important thing, though, was that she was alive! Her body shook as her dad silently patted the shoulders and head glued to his chest.

We stayed that way for a few minutes, silent. Then As'ad gently led his daughter, and we headed back to the church without saying anything. After the priest went into the church and brought back Rula's jacket, we hailed a cab to go home. Rula's face, buried in her hands, and the silent sobs that were still shaking her body kept us quiet.

We didn't find out what happened until after we got her home to her mother and siblings, and after her exhausted body had stopped shivering.

She sat still between her mother and father, gazing at her feet. Her low, monotonous voice reached us as if from a nightmare: "I was on my way home from school. A Mercedes stopped in front of me. I thought it was a cab. There were three men and a woman. Then the woman got out. One of the young men remained in the passenger's seat, and the other two were in the back. 'Abd al-Wahab Street?' I asked the driver. He said, 'Get in.' So I did. He took off like lightning, and at that moment I realized he was headed to the coast. When I opened my mouth, a hand went over it before I could scream. Hands like steel grasped my arms, pulling them behind my back. They blindfolded me, gagged my mouth, and tied my arms behind my back. When I started kicking them, they tied my legs too. 'Move and you're dead!' someone said, and then I could feel a blade on my neck—"

Her mom interrupted, "How many times have we told you not to get in a taxi if there's no other women?"

As'ad looked at his wife reproachfully. The girl said, "There *was* a woman! When she got off, I just thought it was a regular cab. . . . I couldn't move or scream. I just felt the car pick up speed and then go up the mountains. I don't know how high we went or where. When the car suddenly stopped, they pulled me out and took off my blindfold. It was nighttime now, and we were in the woods. They untied my legs. As soon as one of them removed the last rope, I took off running like crazy. I think I caught them by surprise because it took them a minute to realize what had happened. I heard them curse as they ran after me. Thank God it was dark and the place was full of trees. I heard them calling out for me, yelling all sorts of obscenities. Then it seemed as if their voices and footsteps were no longer behind me. They must have gone in the wrong direction, I thought. My arms were still tied behind my back, so when my leg slipped, I rolled down a hill, fast at first, then slower, my clothes getting stuck in thorns. I finally hit a big rock. I was afraid they had heard the noise of the stones that rolled down with me and that they'd find me, so I didn't move. I listened carefully: nothing. Even their voices weren't reaching me anymore, but my heart was beating like crazy. After a while, I began feeling the rocks until I found a rough edge to cut the rope around my arms. Then I kept going down amid the rocks and thorns. I tried not to make too much noise and to stay hidden in the bushes and trees."

We kept looking at the girl as she told her story. No one interrupted her. We couldn't believe she had escaped before they raped and killed her, as had happened to others, and that she was there before us, safe and sound.

"I ran and ran. I don't know where. All I know is that I was going down toward the coast. When I got to the highway, I didn't see anyone, and no one saw me. I crossed the road quickly and walked amid unlit houses until I reached the beach. I was cold. I kept walking. When I found a church, I headed to the door and tried the handle. It was unlocked, so I went in."

A chill must have run through her body, so she stopped talking. Was she recalling the details from last night? Reliving its horror? We remained quiet.

"When I saw the early morning through the windows, I left. I was afraid someone might come into the church and find me, so I went out and walked on the beach."

"Thank God you left your jacket. Otherwise the priest wouldn't have been able to find us."

"I took it off because I was afraid I'd get hot walking on the beach."

She was quiet, then she went on in that same nightmare voice: "I walked for a while, and when I got tired, I went back and sat in the church. When I heard a car in the distance, I ran to the beach so nobody would find me." She was quiet again, and we saw a small smile emerge from her lips. "I don't know why I felt safe at the beach. I just imagined it would be safe, and nobody would see me. I didn't think the opposite might happen."

"We saw you from far, even before we recognized you," As'ad said.

I wondered if she had heard him because she continued: "And when I turned around, I saw three men. My blood froze. They must have followed me! I thought. They've found me! I cursed myself for being stupid and started running. How could I have thought an open beach would protect and hide me!"

"Rula, the important thing is that it wasn't them," As'ad said as he took her in his arms and hugged her. "Just me, Uncle Zahi, and Uncle Sharif."

⁂ ⁂ When Huda opened the door and found Sharif, she froze.

"Is everything alright?"

"Is Dina here?" he asked without crossing the doorstep.

"No, she isn't. Why?" she said. "Come in. Come in. What happened?"

Sharif went in and flung himself on the first seat in front of him, the memory of Rula's story still feeding his fears.

After he told Huda why he was there, she asked, "She's taken her books with her. Do you know who she usually studies with? Who her best friends are?"

For the second time this week, he felt as if he were living next to Dina, not *with* her. "She usually studies alone at home. I know the names of some of her friends—Rima, Wadad, Salima—but I have no idea what their last names are."

"What about her phone book? Did she take that with her?"

Sharif hesitated and said, "I don't know. I hadn't thought of that."

Huda went into her room and came back with her purse. "Let's go find out," she said.

They left.

When Umm Sharif answered the door, she didn't wait for them to ask her, but told them that Dina wasn't back and hadn't called. They ran to Dina's room. It was then that Sharif's gaze fell on top of the dresser.

"Her little bag is gone!" he yelled. He opened her dresser. "And some of her dresses too!"

Huda felt guilty. Had Dina run away because she had told her that there was someone else sharing Sharif's love? Could Huda's desire to have her daughter back be the cause of losing her? Would Dina have run away if she hadn't talked to her about Sharif's love life? How was she so sure Dina wouldn't accept that other woman? Even if Dina didn't, she could still come live with her mother.

"Why did she leave the house?" Sharif asked, standing still in front of the open dresser. Huda didn't dare say anything. With sweaty hands, Sharif opened Dina's desk drawer and started going through her papers: a draft of an essay, old graded assignments, a couple of unused notebooks. Nothing else. He checked her nightstand.

"Here it is!" Sharif yelled. Huda looked at him. He held the little book he had found.

Huda looked at her watch and said hesitantly, "It's ten o'clock! Should we be disturbing people at this hour?"

Sharif gave her the evil eye and without saying anything started dialing a number.

"Sorry to disturb you at this hour, sir, but is Dina al-Mukhtar there? This is her father." Sharif listened to the man's reply.

"Once again," Sharif said, "I'm sorry."

He dialed another number, then dialed it again, Huda's eyes fixed on him.

"I can't get through," he said anxiously and leafed through the little phonebook for another number. And another. And another. Every time he apologized for the disturbance, and he got the same answer every time.

"Maybe she's at the friend's whose number was busy," Huda said. Was she trying to cling to some sort of hope? To feel less guilty?

She said, "Let's try and call from my place."

By the time they arrived at her house, it was eleven-thirty. Fear and anxiety had taken over every other feeling.

She hurried to the phone and dialed a number. It rang for a long time. "Maybe they're sleeping," Sharif said. "Don't hang up. Just wait."

Minutes later a sleepy voice answered. "Hello?"

Her heart beat faster as she apologized. "I'm sorry, ma'am. I'm Dina al-Mukhtar's mother. She hasn't come home, and we're really worried about her. Is she at your house?"

"Dina al-Mukhtar? We don't know this name." She hung up.

Huda froze, the receiver still against her ear.

"What did she say?" Sharif asked.

"They don't know Dina al-Mukhtar."

"Maybe you dialed the wrong number. Give me the phone."

He slowly and carefully dialed the number. It rang for a long time. He waited. A minute. A couple of minutes. Five minutes. The ringing stopped without anybody's picking up.

Sharif put down the receiver and looked at Huda, confused and desperate. "Those were all the numbers in the book."

Huda thought, Could she be at Ramiz's? No way!

"It's midnight, Sharif. Let's wait for her at the school gate tomorrow."

The memory of Rula was still fresh in his mind. "How do you know she'll be at school and that nothing happened to her?" he said.

He grabbed the phone again and dialed a number. "Mom, we couldn't call all of Dina's friends," he said. "We're going to wait for her tomorrow in front of her school. You go to sleep. Don't wait for me."

He put the receiver down and sat still in his chair, studying the carpet at his feet. A minute later he said, "I can't understand why she left the house! We haven't scolded her. We haven't even had an argument with her."

Huda said nothing. She went to the kitchen to make some espresso. Sooner or later he's going to find out why, she thought. She went back to the living room with the espresso, handed Sharif a cup, and sat across from him. She took a couple of sips and, mustering up the courage, said, "I think I know why she might have left the house."

"You do?" He looked at her, surprised and disapproving. "You know, but you haven't said anything?"

"I'm not exactly sure, and I don't know where she might be."

Sharif kept looking at her but didn't say anything. She lowered her eyes and went on. "I suggested she come live with me since there's another woman in your life, and that it would be—"

"So you're the reason!" he interrupted. "As usual, you're the reason behind all my problems! Why should my private life be any of your business? And what does Dina have to do with this?"

He couldn't go on. Anger had knotted his tongue. Huda studied his angry face, his quivering lips. In a tone she tried to control, she said, "Don't be upset,

Sharif, or rant about this. Your private life is not my business at all. In fact, I wish you all the happiness you didn't find with me. But this woman in your life, I'm sure she's expecting you to marry her. That's normal, and—"

"Whether I get married is none of your business, and it won't change anything for Dina. She's my daughter, and she's going to stay with me," he interrupted again, aggressively this time.

His stubbornness got to her. She said, "Don't forget she's *my* daughter too! And she has the right to choose who she wants to live with. If Dina hadn't felt things are going to change for her, she wouldn't have run away."

"I don't see her running to your place!"

She hadn't missed the spite in his voice. "She didn't come yesterday, but she can't stay with friends forever. When I see her, I'm going to talk to her and convince her . . . and please, Sharif, I wish you'd help me. Or would you rather your daughter live with a stepmother?"

"Dina is not going to live anywhere but with me," he said. "Aida knows very well that Dina is my life, and she's going to treat her like her own daughter."

That's what she's claiming now so you'll marry her, Huda thought, but what about later? She didn't say it because she was afraid Sharif would accuse her of being envious and judgmental. Instead, she said, "Right now the important thing is finding Dina and making sure she's okay."

Sharif didn't say anything, and the "couple" remained silent. Then Huda said, "I'm going to make a pot of coffee. Obviously, we're not going to sleep tonight."

She went to the kitchen.

⟵ ⟵ As soon as the arms of the clock signaled seven, Sharif and Huda left the house. They got into Sharif's car and headed to their daughter's school. The gate was still shut, but some children were playing soccer in the yard in front of it. Huda and Sharif stood in front of the gate waiting. When the gate was opened and the students started going in, they studied them, one by one.

"Hey, Rima!" Sharif said, approaching a girl. No, she hadn't seen Dina since she left school yesterday, and she didn't know anything about her. None of the other girls whom Rima stopped to ask about Dina knew anything either. The bell rang, and the students went to their classes. Dina didn't show up.

"Let's go see the principal."

But the principal couldn't help them either. "Call the police," she said. "Maybe she's been in an accident."

Sharif remembered how the police had reacted when he and As'ad had reported Rula missing.

"Do you have the address of a young man called Ramiz? He graduated three years ago. He's a college student now," Huda said.

Surprised, Sharif looked at her, but he didn't say anything. Huda knew what was going through his head. The same thing had gone through hers, but she had doubted it. Still, who knows?

The principal frowned, her forehead wrinkled. She called her secretary. "Nahid, get me the records of our old students." Then, to Huda, she said, "What's his last name?"

"I don't know."

When the secretary came in with a huge, black folder, the principal asked her, "Do you remember a student called Ramiz who graduated three years ago?"

"Which one? Ramiz Haddad or Ramiz Issa?"

"Which one of them is the tall, attractive one, whose father is a rich businessman?"

"It must be Ramiz Issa," she said and opened the folder. Huda wrote down his address and phone number.

Before leaving the school, Sharif said, "Please let us know if you hear anything about Dina."

He couldn't control the trembling in his voice, and the principal could tell he was holding back tears.

"Of course, we'll let you know." What else could she say?

They went to Sharif's house right away.

"I couldn't go to sleep," Sharif's mother said when she opened the door. She had seen her son's car pull up in front of the door. "Have you found out where she is?"

"No, Mom," Sharif said and headed for the phone. He dialed the number and waited.

"Hello. Is this the Issa residence?" he asked. Should he ask for Ramiz? Or Dina? What if Dina wasn't there?

"Yes, it is," a woman's voice replied.

"Is Ramiz home?"

"Who's speaking?"

Sharif hesitated for a moment then said, "Sharif al-Mukhtar. He doesn't know me. Is he home?"

"Dina's father?"

So they did know her, Sharif thought.

"Is she there?" The hope to find her and the wish not to find her there clashed.

Instead of answering his question, the woman said, "Can you come to our house, Mr. Sharif? Here's the address—"

"I already have the address. Has anything happened to her?" he interrupted, frightened.

"Don't worry. She's fine."

"We're on our way!"

He hung up.

"Why didn't she say anything and then just ask you to go there?"

"How should I know?" he said, irritated.

They got out in front of a big villa and followed a sidewalk with bushes and wildflowers on each side. Huda rang the bell. A Filipino maid in an elegant uniform—a white lace headband and a white apron on top of a pink dress—opened the door.

"Sharif al-Mukhtar and his wife. Mrs. Issa is expecting us."

She led them to a living room unlike any they'd seen before. Nayenne carpet spread over bright, ivory tiles; antique-looking tables surrounded modern sofas. On the tables sat figurines made of silver and fine, expensive porcelain.

They remained standing. Huda whispered in Sharif's ears, "How did Dina come to know such a class of people?"

Before Sharif said anything, an elegant woman in her forties came in. She was wearing a gray suit with a maroon blouse and a pearl necklace. That's not a replica, Huda thought right away, eyeing the necklace.

"Have a seat, have a seat," she said, greeting them then pointing to a fancy sofa. They sat next to each other on the edge of the sofa, and the woman sat across from them.

"How do you take your coffee?" she asked as she rang a silver bell on the table to her right.

"We're fine, thanks," they said as if from one mouth.

"We just want to know where our daughter is," Huda said.

The woman gave her a scornful look. "When my husband and I came home at eleven last night, Dina was still here."

Huda tried to defend them both. "We didn't know where she'd gone. We called all her friends—"

The woman ignored Huda's remark and went on. "I don't allow my daughter to stay out all night, so I didn't allow yours to spend the night here as she was planning to."

Huda felt the stab, but she ignored it and said, "Where is she?"

"I told my driver to take her to my mother's. My mother lives alone, so I asked her to give Dina a place to stay until she goes back to you."

It wasn't embarrassment alone that tied Sharif's tongue. He could feel the woman's contempt, her condescension. He tried to hide his resentment as he said, "Thanks for your kindness, ma'am, and your graciousness. Can you please give us your mother's address?"

As soon as the maid closed the door behind them, Sharif said, "The important thing is that we have found her and that she's okay."

"It's not less important for me that she actually resorted to strangers, to rich people who don't have any respect for us or for her, no doubt. I'm sure that woman sent Dina to her mother's to keep her away from her son, so he doesn't get involved with a girl who's not from his own class. That's why she sent her away. I don't think it had anything to do with her concerns about Dina's morals."

She grew silent for a moment, and then she said, "Has Dina realized this now, before it's too late?" She recalled Haifa's face, her lackluster eyes.

A maid opened the door for them and went in to call Dina. They didn't see Ramiz's grandmother.

"She's asleep," the maid had said when Huda asked about her.

"We just wanted to thank her," Huda said. "Maybe you can thank her for us."

Head down, Dina came out with her little bag. She didn't look at her parents or say "good morning." *I hope you've learned your lesson*, Huda thought.

Sharif approached his daughter. He took her bag and hugged her. "Thank God you're okay, sweetheart." He kissed her on the forehead.

That's where your spoiling her has gotten us, Huda thought.

Nobody said anything on the way to Sharif's house. His mother was waiting by the window. She opened the door and hugged Dina.

"You have driven us crazy, sweetie. Where did you disappear? We were going nuts!" she said as she showered kisses on her head, her cheeks, and her neck.

Once again Huda thought: that's where your spoiling her has gotten us! She didn't dare blame or criticize her daughter for fear of putting her off even more.

After carrying Dina's bag to her room, Sharif looked at his watch. "I have to leave you now. I have an important meeting at the office." He looked at his daughter. "I hope you'll be here when I come back!" he said jokingly.

Dina blushed a little as she said, "Of course I'll be here."

When Dina opened her bag, Huda asked, "Why didn't you go to school?"

"I got up late," she said coldly. Was she upset that Huda hadn't kissed and pampered her, as her father and grandmother had done. Dina started putting her clothes back in her dresser, making it clear to her mother that she wouldn't be living with her, no matter what. Huda silently watched her, not knowing what to say. She didn't want to alienate daughter, but she also didn't want her to keep making mistakes.

"Your father and I stayed up all night, Dina. We were very worried about you. All sorts of dreadful thoughts were going on in our heads."

"What could have happened to me?" she said boldly without even looking at her mother as she kept arranging her clothes. Umm Sharif left the room.

"An accident, Dina," she said, "or somebody might have attacked you. We didn't know."

When Dina remained quiet, Huda said sadly, "I had no idea that what I told you would make you run away . . . and to strangers! I treated you as an adult, capable of facing the truth, the truth of life. Otherwise, I wouldn't have told you about your father's relationship with a woman I've known about since . . . well, I thought I was one of the closest people to you, after your father, of course, and that you'd come to me because there's no one else in my life but you. I guess I was wrong. Wrong because I thought of myself as one of the closest people to you, and that you—"

Huda choked on the rest of her sentence and lowered her eyes. She heard Dina move and suddenly felt her arms around her, her body huddling next to hers.

"Mom! Mom! Don't say that!"

Huda hugged her daughter, kissed her, and then moved her back a little bit. "What do you want me to say or think, Dina?" she said. "Can you imagine how humiliated your father and I felt when Ramiz's mother reproached us for your behavior or when she compared you to her daughter?"

Huda saw her daughter's face turn red, so she stopped talking.

A while later Dina said, "I felt embarrassed, too, Mom. It was embarrassing when she sent me to her mother's. She kicked me out of her house, politely."

Finally, it was Huda's perfect opportunity to tell Dina what she had been worrying about since Dina had introduced her to Ramiz. "When you entered their fancy house and saw the maids, did it occur to you that these people wouldn't accept you because you're not one of them? Ramiz is still young, and he may not think that way, but I'm sure his parents do, and when he graduates and goes into the real world, he's going to think just the way they do. I don't want the tragedy of my friend Haifa repeating itself—"

"Haifa? Who's Haifa?" Dina interrupted. Was she trying to change the subject? Rid herself of her mother's blame or of her own guilt?

"Haifa isn't the issue. You are," Huda said. "I can see how you might find Ramiz attractive. He's young, rich, stylish. His social class has taught him good taste and good manners, especially around women. But these are petty things, they don't—"

"Ramiz is very smart," Dina interrupted again. "That's what I like about him."

"I'm sure he's smart, dear," Huda gently said. "That's why he's going to realize it's in his best interest to make his parents happy, especially his father, whose money he's going to inherit years from now."

Huda stopped talking for a minute then said, "You told me yourself that his mother kicked you out politely, so you must have felt unwanted."

Dina had moved away from her mother. She was emptying her book bag and arranging her books and notebooks on her desk. Huda silently watched her for a few minutes, then she said, "Whatever happened happened, Dina.

The important thing is you're back with us, and you're okay. It's a thousand times better that you stay with your father if he gets married—"

"He's not getting married!" Dina interrupted without lifting her eyes from the books she was arranging.

"*If* he gets married," Huda continued as if she hadn't heard her daughter's protest, "and if you are happy with them. You know my house will always be yours and you can come live with me whenever you want."

Dina didn't say anything. Huda got up, stepped closer, and kissed her. She said, "I'm going to leave you now, Dina. You think carefully about what I told you."

Then she left.

15

AT EIGHT ON THE DOT, Najwa was at the door of the medical laboratory. It was shut, so she rang the bell and waited. She didn't hear anything. She rang again and waited. Nothing. She reread the opening hours posted on the door, 7:30 A.M. to 4:00 P.M., and stood waiting. Finally, she heard footsteps on the stairs, but it was just a woman carrying two sacks of fruit and vegetables.

"Doesn't the lab open?" Najwa asked the woman, who was about to go up to the second floor.

"Yes, it does. What time is it now?"

Najwa looked at her watch. "It's a quarter past eight. It says here they open at seven-thirty."

The woman had stopped, catching her breath. "Nobody ever shows up before nine," she said. "Why don't you wait at my place? They usually open at eight-thirty."

"Thanks. I'll just wait here."

The woman went up the stairs, and Najwa sat down on the bottom step, waiting. When the doctor had asked her to get some blood and urine tests, she was told that this lab was "one of the best" and that "all the employees are young university graduates." She wondered as she waited, What about punctuality?

At eight-thirty, a young man showed up. "Have you been waiting for us?" he asked, putting his key in the door.

"For half an hour," she said as she got up. The young man didn't saying anything. He neither explained why he was late nor apologized. When he went inside, she followed him. She handed him the order for tests.

He looked at it for a second and said, "Just a minute. The lab technician will be here shortly, and you can give her your urine sample, too. Why don't you have a seat and get some rest?"

He gave back the order, and Najwa sat down in the chair he pointed to. She was resting from the exhaustion of comfort she'd experienced the past half hour. Then a young woman came in and said, "Good morning, Ziad."

Then she looked at Najwa. "Good morning. Are you waiting for me?"

Ziad answered for her. "She's in here for blood and urine tests."

"Just a minute."

The woman disappeared inside. When Najwa looked at her watch this time, it was a quarter to nine. She almost asked the young man why they didn't change the posted hours since no one showed up before nine, anyway. The woman came out and asked Najwa to follow her, leading her into a small room where Najwa handed the woman her urine sample. The woman sterilized Najwa's arm inside the elbow and took a blood sample. She gave Najwa a cotton ball soaked with alcohol to press against her vein to stop the bleeding. She put the sample in a little glass tube.

"Come by and pick up the results in a couple of days."

Najwa hesitated for a minute and said, "Aren't you going to write my name on the urine and blood samples?"

"I read your name on the prescription," she said. "This is enough. I'll remember."

"But you might get it mixed up with another sample if you don't write people's names on their samples," Najwa insisted.

The young woman looked at Najwa and said coldly, "We know our job, ma'am."

Najwa turned her back and left the room, straightening out her clothes. Another sample of fresh graduates, she thought. She remembered her excitement when she had argued with Huda when they first saw each other. She left the building.

Two days later she went by the laboratory. Her test results were in a sealed envelope with the young man at the front desk. She paid for them and headed to the doctor. Had they sealed the envelope because of the frightening results? she wondered on her way.

The doctor took the report out of the envelope and examined it. He looked up at Najwa, smiled, and said, "Great! Your test results are excellent. What you're feeling is, no doubt, a result of exhaustion."

"Exhaustion?" Najwa said, frustrated. "How can it be exhaustion? I haven't had a job in six months! What—"

"Oftentimes exhaustion can be mental, ma'am," the doctor interrupted. "It might be the result of your not having a job, of your futile job search."

Najwa wasn't convinced. "I'm not a hypochondriac, Doctor—"

"I'm not saying you're imagining pain," he interrupted again. "It is known that a person's mental situation has a big influence on his health—his *bodily* health."

"I know that, Doctor. But what I'm trying to say is I'm not sure the results you just read are mine. They took the two samples from me, but they didn't write my name on them. Maybe they got them mixed up with someone else's samples."

The doctor was in the middle of putting her test results in her file. His hands froze, and he looked at her, bewildered. "Impossible!" he said. "Maybe they just didn't write your name while you were standing there."

"That's not what happened, Doctor," she explained. "The young woman got upset when I asked her to write my name on the sample, and she insisted she could remember it."

The doctor pulled the report from her file and looked at it again. He said, "Some young people, university graduates, have bought the lab from its original owner." He shook his head, and after a moment of silence he said, "In this case, ma'am, I'm going to have to bother you with another test."

"In a different lab!" Najwa said.

"Yes, absolutely," he said. "I'll give you the name of a lab whose owner I've known for a long time."

He wrote down the address. Najwa took it and left. She couldn't control her anger. Isn't it enough I don't have an income or a job and now have to pay twice for these tests, the price of their negligence? She decided to walk home, her tears stinging her eyes and blinding her.

"Najwa!"

She was startled when she heard her name. When she looked up, she saw Huda.

"What's the matter, Najwa?" Huda said. "I tried calling you over and over, but it was useless."

"Our phone has been out of service for three days."

"Oh, well, anyway," Huda said, "they called me from my former school. They need a teacher for French literature and translation."

"Why haven't they called me?" Najwa said. "They have my application."

Huda smiled. "Didn't you just say your phone is out of service?"

"Excuse me, Huda," Najwa laughed, "those people at the lab have driven me crazy." She told her the story. "Now I have to pay for another test," she said.

"'Spend what's in your pocket, and heaven will send some more,'" Huda said and smiled. "See, now heaven has sent you this job. You'll have some income, even if it's just a little, until you find something better."

She grabbed her friend's arms, and for a while they walked together without saying anything.

"I think you're going to enjoy this school," Huda said. "The principal is smart, strong, and humanitarian. She's very keen on the school's academic standards. She hires only serious, qualified teachers, and she really appreciates the devoted ones."

"And these teachers are fine with the low pay?"

Huda grew silent for a moment. "Yes," she said, "either for the same reasons that would make you accept it or because teaching is just convenient for them as mothers. In fact, most of teachers there and in most schools are mothers."

Then, after another moment of silence, Huda said bitterly, "Not all of them are like me. They didn't choose teaching and then get deprived of motherhood because of it."

– 16 –

WHEN DINA ARRIVED HOME from school, Sharif was there, but he was about to leave.

"Are you leaving?" Dina asked, inspecting his clean, ironed shirt, his stylish suit, his shiny shoes.

"I have an appointment, dear," he said and kissed her forehead. She took a whiff of his cologne. She now understood why a few months ago he'd started putting it on before he went out in the evenings.

"You have an appointment every day, Dad! Can't you stay with me just this once?"

"You're going to be studying, dear," he said. "What would I do?"

"A long time ago you used to sit with me and read while I studied," she said, "or you'd tutor me."

Her father laughed as if to lighten the mood. "A long time ago, when you were little, I used to know enough to help you. You don't need my help anymore."

Should she tell him that she needed him to stay and that she needed his love? What was the point when he loved someone else? She kept quiet and didn't lift up eyes to look at him. He withdrew, then gently shut the door behind him. Dina went into her room, grabbed her physics book, and sat at her desk. She opened the book and started reading: "We shouldn't confuse the meanings of the terms "units, *measurements,* and *volume.* Measurement is used to determine the state of a certain object. For example, length is one dimension that can be measured. Similarly, the temperature of a certain object may be considered a measurement of its kinetic energy." Should she go back to her mother? How could she live with her mother every day? She reread the paragraph. No, her father loved her more. Well, he *used* to love her more.

"When we say that the length of a rod is x meters or the temperature of a gas is x degrees, we are specifying the units that we have chosen to designate the length or volume." What does this mean? She closed her book and sat still, staring at the cover. If I go back to Mom, she'll deprive me of the things I like. I won't be able to go the movies whenever I want, go window-shopping with my girlfriends, listen to pop and rock CDs. If only Mom were like Dad! She forces me to read and go to plays and boring concerts. She won't let me do the things I like. I'll die from boredom. My friends will ditch me. No, I'll stay with Dad. But Dad doesn't love me anymore. He sees that woman more than he sees me. He loves her more. Mom loves only me. She loves me, but she doesn't let me do what I want. What if Dad gets married? Would his wife let me do what I want? What kind of a woman is she? Zeina hates her stepmother because she doesn't let her do what she wants and interferes in all her stuff. Is Dad's new woman like Zeina's stepmother? Will she interfere in my stuff? Or will she be too busy with her new husband—her husband who's my Dad? Dad will be too busy with her, too, and they both will leave me alone. What if she doesn't leave me alone, though? Zeina's mother died. I can live with my mother, but Zeina can't . . . or can I?

"This is a great book, Dina. You should read it!" and "Someone told me there's a play in Beirut Theater. Let's go see it," and "I want you to get used to classical music, Dina. There's a concert at the assembly hall in the American University after tomorrow. I'll take you with me." No way! I won't be able to live with her. Should I stay with Dad and the woman I don't know and don't even know anything about?

How long was she to be caught up in this vicious circle of fears?

Her grandmother's voice pulled her out. "Dina, telephone!"

"Who is it?"

"He didn't say."

Her heart beat faster. Could it be him? She hadn't seen him since that day when his mother politely kicked her out of their home. She went to the phone. She was feeling sorry for herself. She had lost her father's love. Ramiz's snobbish mother had separated her from her best friend. Nobody wanted her except for a mother who didn't understand her.

"Hello?"

"Dina?"

"Ramiz!"

Her heart beat faster. She had thought he'd surrendered to his mother's will! She had doubted his friendship, his loyalty!

"Has Zeina invited you to her birthday party today?" Ramiz said.

"Sure. I'll be the first to go."

She heard his silence for a moment before he said, "She's invited me, too, but I'm going to send my regrets . . . another appointment just came up."

"After you've already accepted her invitation?"

As she asked the question, something flashed in her head: his mother must have forbidden him from hanging out with me!

"Yes, it's too bad," he said. "Can you apologize for me? It seems her phone's out of service."

He hung up. Dina remained frozen in front of the phone. Why did he call me just to ask me to apologize to Zeina for him? Or did he just want to find out if I'm going to the party? Because his mother's forbidden him from seeing just me? She felt her face flush with humiliation. Did he notice the excitement in my voice when I said "Ramiz"? Mom was right. He's smart and knows what's in his best interest. He won't upset his parents, his source of wealth . . . like I even care about his money, *their* money.

Her self-pity was mixed with humiliation, loneliness, and resentment.

⸺ ⸺ Friday. Her mother was going to pass by and pick her up. Mom's expecting an answer from me, she thought, but I don't know the answer. I'll just put it off till later. What if she insists? I'll make her wait until the end of the school year or the summer vacation. Dad might leave that woman, or maybe I'll get to meet her. I'm sure he's going to introduce us. She might be more understanding than Mom or less interested in what I do and don't do. Less interested, for sure. Why would she care about me or about my life? She can't order me around. She's not my mother, and I don't have to obey her. All this went through Dina's head as she watched parents pick up their children, one after the other until everybody else had left. She looked at her watch. It wasn't like her mother to be late. Maybe it was the traffic. She put her book bag on the sidewalk and sat on it, waiting. Another half-hour passed, and her mother still hadn't come. Strange! What if something had happened to her? She stood, picked up her bag, and went into the school to call her father.

"Hi, Grandma," she said. "Is Dad home?"

"No, dear. Everything all right?"

Dina was upset. He must be happy that I'm not home to blame him for going out and that he gets to spend more time with *her*.

"Yeah, Grandma," she said. "I just wanted to talk to him."

"Aren't you with your mother?"

She could tell her grandmother was worried. What's the point of worrying her even more? If Mom doesn't show up, I'll just go home as usual.

"Mom called the school and said she was going to be late," Dina said. "It's not a problem, Grandma. Bye!"

She put the receiver down and went out to wait. This time she was anxious. Frightened. Something must have happened to her mother; otherwise, she would have called, as Dina had claimed to her grandmother. If her mother didn't show up by four, she'd go home. But how would she find out if something had happened to her mother?

"How come you're still here, Dina?" The principal pulled her car over and looked inquisitively at the girl.

"I'm waiting for Mom," she said. "She's not here yet."

"When was she supposed to be here?"

Dina hesitated, feeling her face blush. "Two-thirty."

"It's four now!" the principal said, then grew silent, not moving from her place.

Dina guessed what must have been going through her head. "I'm sure something must have come up and she couldn't call," she said. "I'm going home."

Without looking at the principal, she picked up her bag and left. She didn't want to go to her father's house, to face her grandmother's questions, to listen to her recounting her fears or blaming her mother as she usually did. Her grandmother faulted her mother every time Dina voiced a different opinion, every time she refused to drink her milk, every time she gave away a dress she didn't like anymore.

Where was her mother? Whom should she ask about her? For the first time, it occurred to Dina that her mother was, in fact, alone and that if she was in an accident, nobody would find out, and nobody would miss her. Yes, her colleagues and students would . . . when she didn't show up to work. By that time, though, it might be too late to help her. Strangers would miss her, but her husband and her daughter wouldn't know. Her husband wasn't even her husband anymore. What about her daughter—herself, Dina? If she hadn't had an appointment with her, she wouldn't notice that something might have happened to her. What had she found out, though? Just that her mother hadn't shown up. But why hadn't she shown up? Where was she? Whom should Dina ask?

She went into a store. "May I use the phone?" she asked.

The owner of the store was busy weighing some rice for a customer. Without lifting his gaze from the scales, he said, "Go ahead if there's any dial tone."

Dina picked up the receiver and waited. When she heard a dial tone, she dialed her mother's number. As she expected, the phone rang, and nobody answered it. Should she call Uncle Halim since he worked with her mother at the university? She put down the receiver and tried to remember his number. It was useless. She went out. Could her mother have come to the school after Dina had left? She retraced her steps. No one was at the gate. She went in and asked the guard, but he hadn't seen anybody. No one had asked about her. She had no choice but to go home.

There, she turned the key in the lock and opened the door.

"Sharif?" Her grandmother's voice came from the living room.

"No, Grandma," she said. "It's me."

She hurried to her room, grabbed the phone book, and quickly leafed through the pages. Before she left her room to make the calls, her grandmother reached her door.

"What happened?" she asked. "Your mother didn't show up?"

"No, she didn't, and I don't know what happened."

"Didn't she say why she was going to be late when she called the school?"

Her grandmother's questions got on her nerves. Dina said, "She didn't call. I lied to you so you wouldn't worry."

Dina reached for the phone and dialed Uncle Halim's number.

"Hello?" she said. "Auntie Sumaya? It's Dina. Is Uncle Halim home?"

Sumaya sensed the anxiety in the girl's voice. " No. What's wrong, Dina?"

Dina hesitated. "Mom was supposed to come by school today," she said. "I waited for her until four, but she didn't show up"—she choked on the rest of her sentence.

"Halim is in a meeting at the university," she said. "Take his number. Huda might be in the meeting too."

She said that to reassure the girl, but knew exactly what the girl was about to say was logical.

"Why didn't she tell me that," Dina said, "so I wouldn't have waited for her?"

Anger started to take over her fear for her mother.

"I'm sure she couldn't," Sumaya said. "You know how bad the phone lines are."

Dina put down the receiver and called Halim. He picked up the phone.

"Your mom?" he said. "She's not here. She left the university at two. Why?"

Dina didn't answer and put down the receiver. Something must have happened to her mother. But what and where?

Her grandmother was still standing behind her. "What did Halim say?"

"She left the university at two."

She was ashamed for raising her voice. What had her grandmother done for her to yell in her face? She continued in a low voice. "Do you know where Dad went?"

"No," she said. "He just said he was going to be late since you would be with your mother."

He hasn't married her yet, and he's already taking advantage of my absence to stay with her as long as possible. Is she going to let him spend time with me after they're married? "Grandma," she said. "Dad's with the woman he loves. Do you know her name or her number?"

Dina's words made her grandmother's disapproving gaze freeze. "Who told you that, Dina?" she said. "Your father is not in love with anyone."

Dina couldn't help smiling. "Yes, he is, Grandma," she said, "even if you don't know. Haven't you noticed he's been taking care of his looks?"

When her grandmother didn't answer, Dina said, "Mom told me and suggested I go live with her."

The disapproval in her grandmother's eyes turned into anger. "Your mother made that up so she could have you back," she said. "Your mother is responsible for everything that's happened."

"Mom never lies!"

Dina was surprised that she was actually defending her mother. Was it because she was worried about her? Was it because she was upset at her absent father and felt she had no one but her mother? Where was her mother? Where should she ask about her? She grabbed the phonebook, turned to the yellow pages, and called the hospital closest to her mother's university.

"Have you had an injured person by the name of Huda Sabuh?" she asked. "Today, this evening?"

"Are you out of your mind, Dina?" her grandmother asked as Dina waited for an answer from the emergency room. "Why would your mother be in the hospital?"

"Because I can't think of any other reason why she hasn't shown up," she said. "She must have had an accident and was taken to the hospital."

"No, ma'am," the operator said. "We haven't had anyone by that name."

She started calling the emergency units at all the hospitals, one after the other. They said no each time. Her grandmother sat beside her, worry having spread to her, too, but she didn't say anything.

Finally, a different answer came. "One second, ma'am. Somebody mentioned an injured woman being transferred here this evening. Let me check her name."

Dina's heart beat faster. She thought, Can it be Mom? At least I'll know where she is and what happened to her.

"Yes, ma'am. It is Huda Sabuh, but she's not in the emergency unit anymore. She's been transferred."

"Transferred?" she said. "Where to? What happened to her?"

"I don't know, ma'am," the operator said. "I got here ten minutes ago. I just saw her name on the roster. Call the hospital's information line."

Dina put the receiver down, picked up her purse, and told her grandmother, "I'm going to Rizk Hospital. Mom's there."

In the taxi, she visualized her mother with a cast on her arm. No, her leg. If it was anything like that, she'd have been able to call, she thought. She must be unconscious. No, on the operating table. That's why she hasn't called. Dina looked at her watch. If it were a minor operation, it would've been over a long time ago, and her mom would've called. So it couldn't be minor. What if her mother were unconscious or paralyzed?

"Please, hurry."

"Can't you see the traffic, miss? How am I supposed to hurry?"

Finally, she arrived.

"Huda Sabuh, please."

"Room 108."

Dina hurried up the stairs. She cracked open the door to the room. The bed was ready, but there was nobody in it. She went to the hallway, where she stopped a nurse and asked her. The nurse said, "Maybe she's still in the recovery room."

"I'm her daughter," she said. "Please show me where I can find her."

She hadn't thought of asking about the injury until she started hurrying to the recovery room. She saw a nurse coming out of the room and asked her.

The nurse smiled at Dina's worried eyes and trembling voice. "Don't worry," she said. "Thank God, it's minor. It's just a broken pelvis. You'll see her. She's come out from the anesthesia."

When Dina cracked the door, her gaze fell on her mother, who was lying under a white sheet. She tiptoed in and stood by her side.

Huda felt some movement. She opened her eyes. "Dina!" she said in a soft voice, and she smiled without taking her eyes off her daughter.

"What happened, Mom?"

Huda shut her eyes again, the smile not parting from her lips.

"I'm going to stay with you, Mom."

"We're going to transfer her to her room now," a voice said from behind. An orderly approached Huda, grabbed the handles of the stretcher, and gently pushed it outside. Dina walked in front of him. In silence, they reached room 108, where a couple of nurses lifted her onto the bed. One of them covered her, while the other placed a bell next to her head.

"If you need anything, Ms. Sabuh, ring the bell."

They left. Huda's eyes remained shut.

"Are you in pain, Mom?"

"No, I think it's the anesthesia," Huda said in an exhausted voice without opening her eyes.

Dina decided to put off asking her what happened.

"I'm going to call Grandma and let her know you're okay," she said. "Dad's not home."

Her mother didn't open her eyes and said nothing.

Dina called her grandmother, who said her father hadn't arrived yet. "I'm going to stay with Mom," she said. "Don't worry about me." She put down the receiver. Her mother had been looking at her.

"You don't need to do that, Dina," she said. "I'm fine, and you've seen how nice those nurses are."

"I was supposed to sleep over at your place anyway, Mom, so I'm going to!"

Huda smiled at her daughter's firm answer. "Is sleeping at my place so annoying that it's like sleeping at the hospital?"

"Mom, you know that's not what I meant," she said. "I just don't want to leave you!"

"Dear, I know you didn't mean it. I'm just kidding," she said. "You'll get exhausted from sitting here all night. There's no need to do that. Why don't you go home and come back tomorrow?"

"Are you sure, Mom?"

"I'm sure, dear."

Dina bent over her mother, kissed her, and left.

"What happened?" her grandmother asked after opening the door for Dina. Her father wasn't back yet.

"I didn't ask, Grandma," she said. "She was tired. The important thing is that she's okay."

They had dinner. Dina went to her room. She flung herself on her bed and shut her eyes. When Mom goes back home, she thought, she's going to be alone. Did God destine the accident to make me go back to Mom? *Because* it's better for me to go back to my mother? Dad has his new sweetheart, and he has his mother. What about my mother? What about me?

She had no one except her mother. She looked at her watch. It was ten. She got up, slowly took her clothes off, and slipped under the sheets. She felt light, light. In a few minutes, she had gotten rid of the burden of hesitation, the fears of the unknown tomorrow.